A computer expert dating back to the days when computers filled large halls. Now a technology expert dealing with the use of computers in our everyday life leading to smart cities and a greener environment.

Alan Leibert

EARTH TO EARTH

AUSTIN MACAULEY PUBLISHERS™

LONDON * CAMBRIDGE * NEW YORK * SHARJAH

A CIP catalogue record for this title is available from the British Library.

ISBN 9781035810734 (Paperback)
ISBN 9781035810741 (ePub e-book)

www.austinmacauley.com

First Published 2023
Austin Macauley Publishers Ltd®
1 Canada Square
Canary Wharf
London
E14 5AA

Table Of Contents

Prelude

He liked coming home to his family and to his ritual of banging on the front door and saying,

"Guess who is at the door with a present for someone inside."

He always brought a small gift home. He was a fit 30 something, married for five years with a young daughter and a baby son, all of whom he adored. He put the key into the latch and began to turn it but suddenly stopped as a cold shiver ran down his spine. There was no noise, no baby exercising his lungs, no child giggling, no wife calling, something was wrong.

His true name is immaterial, so let's call him Joe for the moment. He earned a better than good living as an independent financial trader, buying and selling whatever looked attractive at the time, all legal – he was a model modern husband. Then there was the other Joe, a ruthless hardnosed money-making machine who dealt indiscriminately with anyone who would pay the asking price, including middle East terrorists, the Israeli defence force, Russian oligarchs, Chinese Tongs and African dictators.

But there was yet more to Joe, under the cover of his successful illegal trading business, there was a yet darker and more sinister side. You have heard of the dark web, the underground internet, he was part of the dark crime. His mantra was simple,

"If you can get it, I don't want it. If you can't get it, I want it."

Everything from missiles to people trafficking and more. As you can imagine, the prices he achieved for his dark market goods were high, very high. Why was he in this business? Partly the thrill but mainly the money. He craved money – lots of it, not for the money itself but for what it could bring – power. He wanted power, dictatorial power, not like the oligarchs or the heads of the major multinationals but more like Stalin or Mao Zedong. He was getting there but not fast enough; he was already over 30.

Joe cautiously turned the key in the lock and pushed the door open. To his horror, standing facing him was a man grinning widely. Joe had never met this man and hoped he never would as he immediately recognised him as Vito Serrano, the world's most vicious, sadistic and psychotic enforcer.

"What have you done with my family?" Joe managed to blurt out.

"Sergei sent me with a message, he doesn't like being ripped off," and with that, he pushed open the door to the ground floor master bedroom. His wife lay naked, tied to the bed, arms and legs spread-eagled and his daughter, also naked, was tied to a chair. There was no sign of the baby.

Joe had long known that one day his triple life would collapse into one and that then would be the time to retire and, he hoped, live happily ever after. He had not expected this. Up till now, all had been going well for him and no one knew he was the master of the dark crime group. In fact, few knew that it even existed and he traded on the rivalry of his customers to keep it that way.

But trouble was brewing. Several of his clients had met quite accidentally at a party and started talking about him. He was clearly playing one off against the other and over-charging where he could get away with it. In particular, a Russian oligarch called Sergei Bucholova had been grossly overcharged compared to the others and declared he would teach him a lesson he would never forget.

Vito Serrano was more than any description could do justice to, anyone who was his target can say goodbye to a normal life from then on. What Serrano did is not discussed here, suffice it to say that Joe had a very painful lesson and sustained life-changing injuries requiring him to spend a month in the hospital and six months' rehabilitation after that. Sergei did not want Joe dead and when he had finished, Serrano left him lying on the floor, conscious and in great pain but completely immobile. Serrano then addressed Joe's wife and child, eventually putting them out of their misery when he had finished. Just to make sure Joe did not bleed out and die, as he left the house, Serrano pressed the panic alarm. The baby was never found.

For his part, Sergei did not know the degree of sadism that Serrano would apply and he fully expected Joe to be back at work as a trader once recovered, but that was not to be. It was two weeks into his hospitalisation and he was beginning to acquire some semblance of consciousness for lengthy periods before he was interviewed by the police when it was confirmed that his wife and child were dead and the baby missing. He had seen it through a fog of pain and blood and hoped it was not true. His life was over, his family killed, his body wrecked and his mind filled with fury.

When he was mended as best as he could be, after recovery had taken place as far as could be, given the nature of his injuries, Joe sold up everything his overt life had stood for and completely dropped out of sight of that life. In fact, he had retreated totally into the depths of dark crime. From this position, he could have done anything he wanted with Serrano and Bucholova, but he decided otherwise. He would go all out to gain his target of unimaginable wealth and the power he craved. As far as his tormentors were concerned, he had other plans for them. Their last nights of untroubled sleep would soon be over. He was, of course, consumed with a sense of revenge and as part of his plans, they would pay, they would all pay.

He had the money and used it to work with experts to design, build and attach various mechanical aids that would allow leading a near-normal life. He added a black face mask and a black hooded cape and began his revenge. Joe was gone forever as he started a new double life, on one side a criminal specialising in dark crime but also an avenger to give vent to his inner rage. He became a one-man vigilante group attacking those who were the worst, those who killed and maimed indiscriminately. In all cases, he killed his targets quickly and without undue suffering. He was not a sadist, just a person trying to clean up the world.

The newspapers loved him, and he was never out of the news, he was the real caped crusader. On the other hand, the authorities took a very dim view of his actions, murder is murder, and he would have to pay. A price of $25,000 was put on his head, but so popular was he that no one even tried to bring him in. The police on the streets did not try very hard to catch him, even if they knew where he was going and what he would do. They would rather let him do his work and escape, leaving the cops to clean up.

He was getting nowhere fast, he could not stem the flow of bad guys with his current strategy. He needed a new approach, one which would address the whole world and its problems as he judged them to be. Perhaps it is an outcome of the ills of the planet, and that is where he must address his actions and give vent to his ongoing anger. He would do better than Stalin who conquered a continent, he would conquer the world.

Sergei Bucholova and Vito Serrano were both worried men. They were sure he was still alive but where and why has he not taken his revenge? For a year they each never travelled without six guards around them. Then they relaxed, he must be dead, and life for them got back to normal. They would soon know the truth. Like the fiction comics, he left a calling card with every victim. It was a white card with black borders appearing to announce a death but his card simply proclaimed,

"Crime doesn't pay," alongside the words a stick drawing of the caped crusader.

Joe Reborn

For the past few years, the weather has become ever more extreme, droughts and floods are now commonplace, temperatures are going up and ice caps are melting causing a catastrophic rise in sea level. We are seeing record severity hurricanes and tornados battering our shores with humankind unable now to do anything about it having wasted years arguing and posturing instead of acting.

The melting ice caps and a corresponding rise in sea level have already engulfed a small Pacific island and several others have had to be abandoned. In the Netherlands, the flood defences, built to last 100 years were overwhelmed during a storm that coincided with a high winter tide and there was extensive flooding, with the saltwater destroying decades of cultivation. The sea was reclaiming its territory. And so it went on across the globe, but it was only when London and New York were flooded that action was taken, albeit too late; it was like King Canute trying to turn back the tide.

As well as expanding the population to unsustainable levels, we know we are also deliberately destroying the planet, or at least making it uninhabitable for humans through encouraging global warming, generating plastics waste, and pollution on land and sea. Is it possible that planet earth itself will wipe out the human population, allowing it to recover over the ensuing million years or so? Will humans reappear as stone-age people and go through the whole cycle once again?

Was the coronavirus Covid-19 pandemic a naturally occurring virus or a man-made one that 'escaped' from a laboratory somewhere in the world, killing indiscriminately, the East, the West, the rich, the poor, the powerful and the weak? There has been non-stop war somewhere in the world for centuries, but it is not enough, even the world wars did not reduce the population sufficiently.

We are in the 21st century in an enlightened society thriving on increasingly rapid technological advances, highly civilised with humankind working collectively for the betterment of all. The above can all be described as true except for the last point. Instead of improving the lives of all, the world today is dominated by those working for their own benefit and glorification. They are the ones who have the money and the power, not the politicians but the owners of very large multinational companies – Apple, Microsoft, Facebook, Amazon and others. The list is not long such that less than 100 people (very largely men) control the world's finances and trade. Are they working together to exercise total dictatorial control over our lives? Not yet but the signs are not good.

At the people's level, kindness has been replaced by race hate, religious fundamentalism, avarice, and greed. The prisons have never been so full, half the world lives below the poverty line and in the last 300 years, there has not been one day without a war being waged somewhere in the world.

We have also reached the point where we have weapons that can destroy planet earth many times over. Can we trust our politicians never to put the world in danger by using these weapons against their enemies?

It is against this background that he, once Joe now the caped crusader, devises his plan. He has spent years planning and considering how he should do it, the 'what' was easy, the 'how' much more difficult. Over the last five years he had been concentrating on acquiring wealth, lots of it, all made much harder by his desire for anonymity which has kept him away from the owners of Facebook, Microsoft and the like. Besides, he knew the dangers of dealing with a combination of more than one of these ultra-rich, ultra-powerful people, he could very well lose control and he was having none of that. His wealth also brought with it considerable power, but he would keep it hidden and use it only when he needed to. The coronavirus has played into his hands, as had the ongoing war between East and West as exemplified by the troubles in Ukraine. All had come at just the right time. He had all the prerequisites and was ready to take his first step. Just one last thing, what he was about to embark on bore no relationship to a comic book hero, the Caped Crusader would have to go.

From now on he would be the controller.

The End

At 7:22 a.m. GMT, 11th November of that fateful year, 15 satellites in low earth orbit at 160km above the earth spread evenly around the equator, fire their engines and begin an unstoppable descent towards earth. After 30 minutes at a height of approximately 30km above ground, each satellite ejects part of its payload and continues its descent to earth, detonating just before crashing into the ground some 8 minutes later.

The payloads ejected at 30km above earth exploded as the satellites approached the ground triggering a massive high-altitude electromagnetic pulse (H-EMP) to be emitted with an effect which was catastrophic. In the first second, the pulse has its maximum effect and takes out all on-earth electronics, planes fall out of the sky killing 100,000s, electricity generation stops, and backup generators don't start, hospital patients hooked up to life-saving equipment die. Elevators stop but do not fall due to safety features – thousands are trapped between floors in pitch darkness. Road and rail traffic stops, even diesels (due to in-vehicle electronics). No communications or computer equipment survives.

The payload in the 15 satellites which exploded when they approached ground were cobalt salted, 100 megaton thermonuclear bombs or H-bombs as they are commonly called. The blast and resulting **shock wave** brings down most buildings, killing millions followed by a **heat wave** killing most of any survivors of the blast as well as triggering **firestorms** across the globe killing millions more, there was no escape. Great plumes of smoke, soot, and dust would be sent aloft from these fires creating thick black clouds which would block out all but a fraction of the sun's light for a period as long as several weeks. The conditions of semidarkness, killing frosts, and **subfreezing temperatures**, will destroy much of what remains of the Earth's vegetation and animal life.

Then, as the nuclear dust falls, **fission products** will kill anyone exposed in the ensuing 30 minutes, with the **fallout** from the cobalt causing long term radiation damage. With a half-life of 52.7 years, it would take 50 years before anyone could venture out for more than a day. After 100 years the radiation would be negligible.

It is 8 a.m. on D-Day.

The end.

Book 1
Realisation

STP Industries in many ways was a typical tech start-up, rags to riches in just a few years and of course based in California. But no, this start-up hails from Helsinki in Finland although it is true that sometime after launching in Helsinki, it did set up a not insignificant facility in California.

It started with just one man, Michael Kowelski, an American citizen of history and origin unknown. He delighted in being completely open with a crowd and yet telling them nothing,

"We are going to change the world, solve global warming, and bring good to all humankind. Our products will be like nothing you have ever seen," he told them without telling them what the products were.

"Just wait and see," he liked to say, hinting that he also did not know what they were.

After a year in the job, he was still as much an enigma as the person who had suddenly turned up from nowhere to head what in a short space of time, had become a major player in the tech industry.

Michael must, at some point, have been told about the products STP Industries was going to produce, because he changed tack overnight and appeared to be completely open about what the company was doing,

"Listen well and take note," he would say, "We are building a whole range of planet-friendly products from wave-hopping, energy-efficient planes to advanced battery technology for powering motor vehicles and much more."

Michael Kowelski was a good showman, able to hold an audience for an hour or so on his own wowing the crowd and telling all who would listen to everything about STP Industries pending significant achievements in terms of the products it would be introducing in the coming few years. And indeed, they were significant and many, so much so that few believed it and enjoyed listening to Michael Kowelski talking and making what seemed to be wild claims. How wrong they would be proved to be.

Quite why the start-up was in Finland nobody knows, and Michael Kowelski was just as circumspect and would say,

"We are based in Finland because that is where our backers wanted it to be. Surely you can understand that Finland is exactly the type of country that fits our remit as a planet-supporting company. Even the name STP Industries fits our objectives if you assume STP means 'Save the Planet', what else can it mean?"

In some ways, to prove the point he recruited his first board and top-level management including some noted scientists. At the same time, he recruited some more dubious characters to the board. All in all, the birth and early development of the company can only be called strange, yet it had what seemed to be an endless pool of money allowing Michael Kowelski to recruit a number of top-flight engineers and scientists of all disciplines.

STP Industries had opened a large facility in Palo Alto Southern California which turned out to be the company's main research, development and production facility to which those recruited were transferred. The Helsinki facility became the head office and administration centre and apart from Michael Kowelski's apparently open pronouncements to the press, the office in Helsinki became a highly secure stronghold for the company. It intercepted all requests to any office of the company and stone-walled all attempts at gaining further information about the company, whether in person or electronically, no-one was able to break through the outer shell of security and many tried.

There was also a rumour circulating that STP Industries had opened a third facility in the Outback of central Australia but this was vigorously denied and so far, no one had managed to locate it or prove any link to any shack or shed found. This was aboriginal land and anyone working in any field of tech would be mad to start up anything there, especially after Australia had given the aboriginals rights over their land and its use. So, a rumour remained a rumour except in the mind of a few conspiracy theorists who doubted STP Industries' intentions.

Oddly, no sooner had the conspiracy theorists gained any sort of a hearing, they stopped their campaigning and disappeared, giving rise to a whole new raft of conspiracy theories, the most popular being that STP Industries was a front for a secret US Government agency, but to do what? And why start in Finland? Aliens were even mentioned.

Working for STP industries was seen to be a top job paying good money and working on exciting projects and yet employees quickly changed their demeanour after joining the company. Previously outgoing people became quiet, morose and at pains not to talk about their work, even to their peers. What little was gleaned from a variety of journalists who had deep pockets and were happy to grease palms to get a good story was that employees working on one project were not permitted even to say hello to employees working on another. Break the rules in or out of work and you were out, and out meant out. Rumours and 'facts' were circulated such that you could not easily get another job in California. Besides, many support companies made a good living by supplying STP Industries and they did not want to risk alienating them by hiring those whom STP Industries had fired. There was no 'three strikes, and you are out' rule.

In just two years, STP industries had set up and started work in two large facilities, perhaps three and had hired several hundred staff but so far had produced nothing and not raised any money on the open market. Someone with deep pockets must be in the background, but who? What was it all about? The world would soon find out.

Tony Silbeck

Rhino was a virtual world name to be feared by all, especially the rich and global companies. In the real world he, or was it she, had no name, no one knew who Rhino really was, so he or she would have to be 'outed' or stopped in the virtual world if Rhino's criminal escapades were to be reined in, but no one had come even close, even with the $20m price put on Rhino's head by a group of multi-national companies.

Rhino was an indiscriminate, brilliant hacker who, without thought of the possible consequences, would close and drain an oil company's bank accounts bankrupting it overnight; publish details of all Twitter account holders; open the ballistic weapons silos of the USA, and so on. Rhino did not care, the more trouble he caused, the more fun there was to be enjoyed. Rhino was a psychopath and a brilliant one, which is why the controller wanted him.

At the age of six, Tony Silbeck was already in trouble. He had lived on the streets with his mother for as long as he could remember and now his mother was dead. For the last month, he had gone around with a gang which he enjoyed. He had company, food in his mouth and somewhere to sleep. But the gang had seen him as a revenue-earning commodity and offered his services to the various perverts cruising the streets at night.

Tony did not know what this was all about and received a painful and shocking introduction. After the third night's work, he ran away from the gang and was on the streets on his own again, hungry and cold. He began stealing food from shops in the town but was not very good at it and always got caught. Local justice was the byword and over the next few months, he received regular beatings. Beatings teach they say, and Tony Silbeck learned, not right from wrong, but to be on the side of the beater, not the beaten. This philosophy coloured his whole life from then on – win at all costs regardless of the effect on others.

Eventually, he came to the notice of the Local Authorities and was placed in an orphanage where he spent the next nine years. He did not enjoy this period in his life but did not run away as he remembered his time on the streets; here he had warmth, food and clothing. He proved to be highly intelligent, both in the normal sense and in his ability to manipulate people. He made no friends and did not participate in group activities and sports. But he was not lonely, he had the Internet.

Early on in his stay at the orphanage, his class teacher introduced him to computing and the Internet in the hope of getting a positive reaction and finding something the boy could enjoy and interact with. It turned out that he had a penchant for computing, and rapidly outstripped the capabilities of anyone at the orphanage. From then on, he did not divulge what he was doing on the Internet except to help the orphanage and make them grateful enough to allow him to do what he wanted when he wanted, which was most of the time. He mechanised the orphan's information site, designed and implemented their accounts and set up links to all external agencies. In dealing with them, he manipulated the data just enough to make the orphanage look good without raising any eyebrows of doubt.

His own activities involved looking at Web sites and at how payments were made for goods and services. He learned to become a thief by taking payment for the sale of non-existent goods. Since he did not inform the person whose money he took that he had sold them something which he did not deliver, for a long time no one cottoned on to what he had done. He was surprised to find how few people checked their bank records down to every line item. Eventually, someone became concerned and the police computer crime unit became involved.

He stopped his scam immediately, rerouted his access via a different service provider and changed his name, at least on the Internet. But by now he had more than £50,000 in the bank. Nevertheless, he had learnt an important lesson, not to get caught. He had been alright when staying under the radar and only stealing small amounts but at risk of being caught when he upped his take to such a level that his targets were bound to notice the scam and call the police. Of the utmost importance, he had to make sure that whatever he did on the Internet, he could never be identified. So, he took the name Rhino for his virtual presence and piggy-backed onto other websites when carrying out traceable activities. This allowed him to steal whatsoever he wanted and whenever he wanted.

At the age of 15, he left the orphanage to start making his own way in the world. Over the coming year or so he joined and worked for an Internet Service Provider, a video games producer and a pornography website manager – all to learn his trade and better his knowledge, becoming the best in the world. Unfortunately for the rest of the world, being the best in the world went to his head. He no longer hid but promoted the fact that he was Rhino who had done whatever had been done. He became notorious for causing havoc on the Internet – stealing money, corrupting sites, encrypting and ransoming organisations, breaking into secure government sites, exposing secrets – so much so that a price of $20 million was placed on his head. No one claimed the bounty although many had tried to.

Unexpectedly, he received an email from someone offering him a job.

"Dear Rhino, I have studied your exploits over the past few months and decided that you would fit in well in our organisation. Terms would be generous, although I know you do not need more money, please reply to his email address which will remain active until midnight tonight. After that, just post 'yes' or 'no' on Twitter's home page. I realise you are not authorised to do this, but I am sure this will present no problem for you.

Don't wait too long, I look forward to you becoming a key part of our team."

Was this a trick to draw him into the open? He tried to get some background on the approach and came up with a blank. These people were clever, maybe almost as clever as Rhino. Intrigued, he wanted to respond and learn how they did it, ghosts were not allowed on the Internet. However, having learned his lesson a few years ago, he did not want to risk it again and decided not to respond.

About a week after his last attempt at tracking down where the job offer had come from, a letter arrived at his flat, addressed to Tony Silbeck – nothing unusual in that, to the real world he was Tony Silbeck. But what the letter contained both shocked and scared him. It read simply,

"Rhino, please respond to my job offer". He had been found out. He had no choice now, he had to respond. Waiting on his computer was another message from the same source (which he assumed but could not prove). The approach was by a start-up company called STP Industries which had found Rhino but had not exposed him or claimed the bounty. He was intrigued by what he was told about the company's plans and that he was offered a directorship, but the clincher was that he would be employed as Tony Silbeck and be left alone to carry on his own activities as Rhino without any connection to Tony Silbeck. Tony accepted the offer.

So far so good, one more piece in the jigsaw that was the controller's grand plan. He sat back, satisfied – a perfect start. He was a patient person who had as much time as it took and he already had two psychopaths working for him, both at the very top of their profession, Serrano who did not know it yet and Silbeck aka Rhino.

D-Day Minus 4 Years

It is D-Day minus 4 years. A man, or is it a woman, sits down with a clean sheet of paper. The person writes. Heading – Constituent Requirements. Underneath the person writes a list:

- The anarchists
- The tree huggers
- The scientists
- The technologists
- The producers
- The hackers
- The rich
- The politicians

The person returns to the top of the page and crosses out the heading and replaces it with the words:

"**The controller**" adding underneath "**Pre-requisite skills**".

It had begun and nothing can stop it until it has reached its conclusion.

Three weeks later a new company was formed in Helsinki, Finland – STP Industries which was widely touted as meaning Save The Planet. It had only one employee, the CEO, Michael Kowelski who took every opportunity to meet the press and talk about STP Industries' aims and ideals which were broadly to save the planet through technology operating in all disciplines.

Recruiting began, strictly by headhunting specific people, starting with the Board of directors:

-Michael Kowelski	Unknown	CEO
-Sir James Scott	Politician	Chairman
-Sergei Bucholova	Rich	Finance Director*
-Vito Serrano	Mercenary	Director of Security*
-Gen. Jim Bray	Soldier	Director of Marketing
-Tony Silbeck	Hacker	IT Director*
-Prof. Wu Lee	Physicist	Research Director
-Raymond Carver	Technologist	Production Director
-Claud Liphook	Environmentalist	Planetary Director
-	Not appointed	Sales Director

* Known to and directly recruited by the controller.

The Helsinki facility was clearly just a head office sited as far away from the 'boiler house' as possible, at least as far as American thinking goes. The boiler house was soon acquired, and it was placed just about where everyone thought it would be, in Palo Alto, Southern California, set to be STP Industries Research, Development and Production facility. Raymond Carver was assigned to this facility but not manage it, this job was given to Ernst Wiegand, a proven tech start-up manager. Raymond Carver did not mind, he was being paid enough not to mind. Besides, he knew that he would soon be ruling the roost, he had that reputation.

Tony Silbeck was already known as being on board as indicated by the asterisk next to his name and the type of character he was set the tone for the whole board. Vito Serrano and Sergei Bucholova, both also asterisked, were two major surprises, The controller was not yet ready to exact his revenge on them, but he made sure they knew who he was and that he would act if they did not join STP Industries, keep secret who he was and do whatever he asks of them. They agreed, besides which they were being paid a lot of money in a legitimate business. However, they would never stop looking over their shoulder. The controller was content with this arrangement, the boot was now on the other foot.

The first Board meeting was a formality and turned out to be the only one attended by the whole board.

"Welcome to the STP Industries Board," started Michael Kowelski, "I am Michael Koweslski and I am your CEO, I propose we go round the table and introduce ourselves. I will start with the gentleman on my right, your name and role please."

"Vito Serrano, Security." "Sergei Bucholova, Finance." "Tony Silbeck, IT."

"Sir James Scott, Chairman." He did not seem worried that Michael Koweslki had ignored him and was chairing the meeting. Anyway, he knew damn all about the company.

"Jim Bray, Marketing and Public Relations." He deliberately dropped off the 'General' and had pointedly sat as far from Serrano as possible.

"Claud Liphook, environment." "Wu Lee, Research."

"Ray Carver, Production." Michael Kowelski continued,

"Thank you, gentlemen, there will be no other business to discuss today and I will leave you to get to know the company, your role and each other. Any and all questions should be directed to me. So, thank you all for coming and I now close the meeting." And that was that.

A third facility was rumoured but not confirmed. It was claimed by some as being in Ulara in the southern part of the Northern Territory of Australia, about 15 km from Uluru and 100 km East of Alice Springs. Professor Wu Lee had disappeared soon after he was wheeled out. It was thought he was assigned to work there.

Over the ensuing few months all the usual staffing positions were filled, and it became clear that this start-up was no small enterprise although what it was doing, researching, producing and planning to sell was unclear. The brains of California rushed to its door trying to join the company and many lived to regret it.

There was no hard evidence as to what was really going on at STP Industries except that it was high-tech, leading edge. It could be in any sector, but the rumour mill had it being all of space research, clean energy, new computing technology, AI and high-speed communications. It could also, just as easily be something entirely different, the only clue being the press conference pronouncements of Michael Kowelski and the specialities of those hired, but the indications were that it was in some way, multi-disciplinary. Such a multi-discipline operation would take vast amounts of money and major manpower resources, which, for a start-up with no visible external funding, just could not and was not believed.

The more they were stone-walled, the more the press became interested, only to be rebuffed at every turn. The employees were not talking, the company through Michael Kowelski was just giving out platitudes indicating that when they are ready, all will become clear, and they will be pleasantly surprised at what is announced. After a while, the press realised that he knew little more than they did, making him the ideal spokesperson for the company.

Professor Wu Lee

Professor Wu Lee was Chinese and a genius nuclear physicist. He could make a bomb capable of killing 100,000 people blindfolded and with one arm tied behind his back and therein lay the problem; self-centred Wu Lee would stop at nothing to achieve whatever target he had for the day or month or year. He did not care how many his bomb would kill so long as it worked according to its design specification, neither below it nor above it. He had all the classic signs of Asperger's Syndrome and also being psychotic, another ideal candidate for the Board of STP Industries.

However, all was not good on the Wu Lee horizon. Last year, while working for the foremost nuclear research facility in China, he commenced an experiment to create nuclear fusion. He was excited, he knew how to do it and all that eluded him were the mechanics that would start and stop the process – leave it running in its present state and it would switch the process from fusion to fission and bang! His department head scheduled Wu Lee's next test in six weeks and knowing of the power it demanded, arranged to tell the nearby town that their power might go off for an hour or so when this test was being carried out, but if it worked, it would be the greatest invention since the wheel, and they would have been part of it.

"Not good enough!" shouted Wu Lee but to no avail, it would be in six weeks. "Over my dead body," he mumbled under his breath and without telling anyone, in two days he was ready.

That evening after everyone had gone home for the night, feigning a heavy workload he went back to his lab and started his experiment. Power was lost for 20 miles around his lab and since the repair men had not been pre-warned, it was seven hours before power was fully restored, during which time three people had died in hospitals, five had died in road crashes and 120 people in a plane in the process of touching down when the runway lights suddenly disappeared. Wu Lee was not sorry for the loss of life, only that the experiment had failed and not that he had nearly blown the facility to kingdom come when the power started failing for him.

Despite protestations that he was very close to success, he was summarily fired on the spot. After his uncontrolled actions had been made public, no one 'legitimate' would hire him and he turned towards the middle East terrorist factions but stopped short when he received an offer from a start-up company called STP Industries to join them.

"Dear Professor Wu Lee,

We are mightily impressed by your work in nuclear fusion technology and would like to offer you a job continuing that work as well as carrying out other tasks for me. Please reply with your decision which I sincerely hope will be yes."

Attached to the email was a contract including employment terms and an offer of a directorship. He jumped at the offer and joined the first Board Meeting of STP Industries in Helsinki, Finland but was told that he would be working out of their new facility in California. In reality, he was flown to the middle of nowhere in Australia, worked to his limit on STP Industries nuclear bomb manufacture and had almost no time for his own research. There were no weekends, no days off and no time outside the facility. The only diversion he had was the girl they had given him as his own personal possession to do with as he wished, which he did but that did not satisfy him, he wanted to complete his fusion process.

What surprised him was that for a green, fighting climate change company, STP Industries showed little interest in his nuclear fusion work, even though he had laid it out for them in detail and showed that he had solved the problem he had on his last test. He did not mind telling them all about his work as he knew he was the only one who could make it happen; he was sure of that.

Wu Lee was now part of the controller's plan, a key part and another piece in the jigsaw and with the right temperament, not psychotic but single-minded without regard to the consequences,
He will do, he will do very nicely, thought the controller.

Chess Chessington

In the digital world, security is paramount. Companies strive to protect their data, new companies, often set up by hot-shot college graduates, aim to provide the tools to achieve a secure environment, while hackers show how easily security can be breached, either maliciously or benevolently.

It is all a big game, a very lucrative game, it is a game of leapfrog, a new system, scheme or methodology is produced, companies acquire it, hackers break it and so it goes on. It is a game of stable doors being closed after the event and ever bigger brick walls being climbed over by the hackers.

The only real solution is,

"If you don't want to be hacked, don't go online".

In this background. SAGE was formed some four years before as a security agency. It was as much concerned about people as technology and for once in this business sector, it was an honest company. It was headquartered in Palo Alto in California, not far from STP Industries.

It worked mainly for large organisations and was known for its honesty and pulling no punches. In its short life, it had found as many rogue employees as it did digital timebombs.

SAGE was headed by Chester (Chess) Chessington who, together with his two right-hand best and most trusted employees, Jim (the Weasel) Waverley and Tamantha (Tam) Sturrage covered all the bases. Chess is a people person who could smell out the most trusted client company employee who was cheating on the company. TAM is a computer genius having been an elite club hacker for five years, then working for those unnamed government agencies you know exist but have no evidence whatsoever. She had been caught hacking and the choices given to her were to work for them or go to jail – she chose the former. Thanks to efforts by the head of SAGE, Chess, Tam was now working for SAGE and at last happy with her job. She was not a small woman and had a character to suit, so for her, clandestine work was out but then her job was one of operating behind the scenes.

"Why chase when you can control every CCTV camera in the city and control all the traffic lights."

The Weasel was quite the opposite, so normal and nondescript that he would simply melt into any crowd and move around unnoticed. He was the architype private dick, a Philip Marlowe, only the Weasel made no show it. He did not want accolades or a reputation, in fact, he actively shied away from the limelight, he wanted to remain unnoticed, and he was very good at it.

SAGE supplies consultancy services mainly to large organisations country-wide but with most businesses coming from Southern California where the tech-savvy good boys and bad boys tend to congregate, and business was good. They had a reputation for honesty and telling the unvarnished truth. The combination of Chess, Tam and the Weasel gave them all the expertise they needed in both the real and the virtual worlds. Tam and the Weasel each led a team of almost-as-good consultants, but they were running at over 90% loading and were recruiting hard.

They did not have time for speculative investigation and only registered mild interest in STP Industries because they were also recruiting and offering salaries over the market rate. Luckily, they were not after people with the skills SAGE required, however, their action did push the salary requirement up across the board.

He tried hard to hate his parents for naming him Chester, but they were too nice, and he loved them dearly. They were both in their 80's now and remained in good health, and as a result, he hoped the food they fed him in his youth will see him in equally good stead when he reaches that age. He also realised now what a good choice of name his father had made; nobody forgets the name Chester Chessington.

Chess was ex-army, initially heading a tank division but then moving into military intelligence, a job which he loved. He had continued to keep 'army fit' and at six feet one inch, he was an imposing man. He had retained his army haircut and although he had been out more than five years, he was clearly 'army'. He had an army wife, the daughter of a long-term army sergeant, who loved Chess dearly and willingly followed him wherever was posted around the world. Unfortunately, when he was on a tour of duty with his tank division in Iraq, a stray shell of unknown origin landed in their compound and killed his wife, his young son, and their unborn child. Although consumed with rage, he kept his head and vowed to find out which group had fired it. His colleagues urged him to kill everyone against them, but Chess was having none of it and he approached the problem with meticulous analysis and logic.

He began to be concerned when information stopped being given freely to him. He eventually found out that it was a friendly, US army shell that had hit the compound. His problems got worse when they tried to sweep it under the carpet, and he came up against an impenetrable closed door of generals who did not want the embarrassment and shame to dirty their uniforms. Dogged determination resulted eventually in the retirement of three generals, all without a stain on their characters. One lowly corporal took the blame for firing the shell, something which he has always denied, and was jailed for five years and dishonourably discharged. It was these events that made him leave tanks and join intelligence.

However, he retired from the army when his tour of duty ended, finally disillusioned by the politicising of the army; now they fought strategic wars to get their man in power. And where there was no war, they would create one. He had had enough and when the next head-hunter approached him, he accepted.

Out of the frying pan into the fire! He joined a major international company as head of security only to find the political moves even worse. But what got to him was the industrial espionage that he was expected to join in with. He left after three months and decided on going on his own and honestly. So, he founded SAGE.

SAGE's encounter with STP Industries over recruitment aroused his curiosity and although they were too busy on revenue-earning activities to look too closely, Chess took it upon himself to do a little investigating. He looked at the Board and did not like what he saw. Something bad was going on there which he would have to park until he could investigate properly and quietly. He would wait until Tam and the Weasel were free.

Tony Silbeck aka Rhino was happy, he was causing sanctioned mischief as well as doing his own thing. Having wiped out the bank accounts of those he had decided had disrespected him, he had no further need for accumulating money and set about his most enjoyable activity, breaking into secure systems and not just leaving a calling card but wreaking havoc with the systems he had broken into. He had already broken into all the major defence sites in the world, taking control of army drones and causing them to hit the "wrong target". But he was being more circumspect about breaking into the US NSA site, which all hackers regarded as the ultimate challenge.

He was right to be wary for they were waiting for him. He could have entered through any one of several weak points he had observed. He was frankly amazed at how leaky the site appeared to be which should have rung warning bells in his head, but his arrogance told him he could do no wrong. So, for the first time in his career, he fell straight into a trap. His target shut down all access except his entry comms link which it used to backtrack through Rhino's circuitous route to the NSA. Then that link was broken and the whole site shut down – it was a gigantic fake created just to entice Rhino in.

Rhino was beside himself with a combination of anger and embarrassment. He had to call someone in STP Industries to ask for time off and if possible, somewhere to hide. What about the mysterious Australian facility? He flew to Helsinki and called the top man in the organisation, Michael Kowelski but he was worse than useless saying he would refer it up and Rhino should stay put and wait.

"Up where?" asked Rhino who thought he had reached the top. It was three days now and Rhino was amazed he was still alive, but he was. Michael Kowelski called him at his hotel and asked him to come into the office. There, he was put in a video conference theatre and left all alone, not even Michael stayed. A conversation started with an individual who had switched his camera off.

"Rhino, yes I know who you are, you have been a really stupid man. A most important lesson to learn is to know your enemy." He started and then continued,

"Because you are valuable to STP Industries, I have squared your misdemeanour with the powers that be. So, you are free to continue your dangerous pastime so long as you stay away from the NSA and a number of key sites around the world that I will inform you of from time to time. I may also ask you to kill or disrupt a site from time to time."

Rhino was shocked, who was this? Who knew who he was? Who had the power to control the NSA? It could only be someone high up in the US government or at the top of the NSA. Either way, he was a lucky man, buoyed up by the thought of his own very powerful fairy godfather. He caught the next plane to San Francisco and by the time he got off the plane, all sense of fear had left him far behind. He was walking up the airport concourse, passing a set of telephone booths when one of the phones opposite him rang. Out of curiosity, he answered it, "Hello Rhino, welcome back, sorry to catch you off guard but I remembered I have neglected to tell you my name, most remiss of me. They call me – the controller." The phone went dead.

Chess looked at the list of STP Industries Board with incredulity. What brought this set of dysfunctional people together and made them board members of a well-financed high-tech organisation? What was STP Industries and who was running it? Looking at the Board it was clear that the company was no ordinary organisation.

Of those he knew, they were a motley lot including at least one active criminal. He sat down at his desk and made a list, looking up those he did not know.

Name	Profession	Nationality	Role at STP Industries	Chess's Comments
Sir James Scott	Politician	British	Chairman	Resigned UK parliament under a cloud
Sergei Bucholova	Financier	Russian	Finance Director	Oligarch who made his money out of the misery of others
Vito Serrano	Mercenary	Italian	Security Director	A sadistic thug to be avoided at all costs
Gen. Jim Bray	Soldier	American	Marketing Director	Disillusioned at politics being brought into the armed forces of the world
Tony Silbeck	Hacker	Unknown	IT Director	Would work for anyone who would keep him out of gaol and leave him alone on his computer
Prof. Wu Lee	Scientist	Chinese	Research Director	A clever nuclear scientist apparently sacked for selling nuclear technology to the mid-East (but the truth was other) otherwise)

Raymond Carver	Engineer	South African	Production Director	A reputation for getting things done by being a bully
Claud Liphook	Environmentalist	American	Planetary Director	Passionate about saving the planet. What was he doing in such bad company
Michael Kowelski	Unknown	Unknown	CEO	Unknown but appears to revel in the limelight

Conspicuous by their absence were the women. In these modern times, it is almost mandatory to have at least one woman on the board. Chess surmised that this was because the company was very much a 'Macho' company and the 'mine is bigger than yours' syndrome does not apply to women.

Chess was struck with horror when he thought of Professor Wu Lee working with probably the world's most vicious sadistic thug, Vito Serrano. Wu Lee was perhaps even more dangerous in that his actions could kill millions of people as well as start World War 3. So, are we looking at a nuclear holocaust in the Middle East? Or would the world be held to ransom by the thugs? However, his knowledge was such that rather than kill Wu Lee, countries big and small sought to control him.

With these people on the board, it was amazing to Chess that Claud Liphook was also on the board. He was well known across the world, and he would certainly bring press coverage with him. To Chess, this board structure did not seem quite right – another question in the STP Industries file for future reference.

Chess turned his attention to General Jim Bray. He had had an excellent and rewarding career in the army but had very publicly expressed his disillusion at the politicising of the army, just like Chess. On the general front, he took issue with the army being used at political rallies and by implication siding with the 'flavour' of the speakers. Like Chess, Jim Bray took a civilian job and again like Chess, he left after three months disillusioned at the industrial espionage he was expected to carry out. Jim however, having worked his way to general from private, felt he had a good story to tell, and he started on his autobiography. So, mused Chess, why would an honest, straight-up hero be working for STP Industries? What was the general doing here sitting around the same table with Serrano?

Who was Tony Silbeck? Chess had never heard of him and all efforts to find out anything had come back blank. Clearly, someone had erased all his records – no birth certificate, no passport, no driver's licence, no nothing. He did not know why Silbeck was hired but he deduced from the lack of information available and consequently based on what Tony Silbeck must have done for himself and others, that he was some sort of computer genius. He asked Tam what she could find out, but she also came back with a blank with one small, but as they found out later a vital exception. There was a legendary computer hacker known by the codename "Rhino" who was indiscriminate in the havoc he caused, so much so that industries around the world had clubbed together to put a price of $20 million on his head for his exposure but after nearly a year no-one had come close. Tam had found some indication that Tony Silbeck may be Rhino and if he was, she would be no match for him.

It seemed that Michael Kowelski must have been helped by Tony Silbeck to lose his past. Michael was clearly a frontman and Chess did not waste too much time on him especially as he was not a shareholder of STP Industries. Chess was determined to find out who was behind the company, why it was set up the way it was and what its aims were. A cold wind blew past his face, suddenly he was very scared. It was Tam who first heard a new name associated with STP Industries, a piece of computer data that had been marked for shredding and destruction but after delivery to its destination and decrypted for the recipient, had been left lying around and not destroyed as it should have been. The name was the controller.

D-Day Minus 3 Years

STP Industries was now an established operation, headquartered in Helsinki but that was just a showy head office with all the real work going on in Palo Alto, California. Every day, millions of dollars were being pumped into the company with nothing to show for it after three years. Someone somewhere had very deep pockets.

Michael Kowelski was based in Helsinki with a small administrative staff. His main function was to deal with the press, which was an ideal strategy for the company as he knew nothing which meant he could not tell the press anything new except some rah-rah words he was given just before each press conference.

Based on the notes he received, Michael had recently started to hold more frequent press conferences at last explaining to the world what STP Industries was doing. Now the company was up and running, he could talk about their research on nuclear fusion, remote sensing, carbon capture, plastic breakdown, battery technology, solar power, wave hopping planes, etc. if this was true, it would be an enormous and diverse undertaking eating up a tremendous amount of money – whose money?

The press loved the press conferences mainly because they did not believe a word of what Michael was saying about the research coming to fruition and products being delivered soon. But Michael kept saying his favourite phrase,

"You ain't seen nothing yet."

The press delighted in picking up on that and ridiculed him with,

"So STP Industries is going to do what a dozen other companies have taken years trying, and in the process, spent vast amounts of money, and yet failed to achieve just one of the products, let alone all of them. Let's rename the company 'Miracle Industries' and you 'the Saviour'."

Nonetheless, research projects and upcoming products were all that Michael would talk about. He refused to acknowledge that the Australian operation existed, refused to talk about ownership, where the money was coming from, or about some mysterious staff disappearances. He even refused to talk about his own Board and some of its more dubious directors.

It became clear that Michael Kowelski was just a frontman and that Helsinki had been chosen because it was a long way from California. Then there is Australia; the press had even been there and were quietly but firmly turned away. Drones were tried and shot down. Michael Kowelski still refused to acknowledge ay presence in Australia.

Once fully operational, the company's organisational structure was to divide it into specific unnamed product divisions each operating entirely independently with staff confined to their own areas and projects and warned not to talk about their work to employees in other divisions. By taking this approach, they had to duplicate quite a lot of expertise that could have been used by more than one division, but the company nevertheless kept to its rule of each staff member working for just one division. Yet the press was invited to tour the facilities and publish what they saw and heard. The result was that no one besides the controller knew the end game. All thought it was something else.

There were few Board meetings with most directors dialling in on conference calls; the full board never got together face-to-face again.

The press being the press would never leave a good story alone and the less they knew, the more interested they became. Their attitudes broke into three distinct groups:

- Facts that they knew: there was little of this and it was mainly restricted to the scientific press.
- Speculation: taking what little they knew and extrapolating to reasonable possibility. This included the main bulk of the newspapers and magazines.
- Wishful thinking: anything to sell newspapers and restricted to the sensationalist and exposé newspapers and magazines.

The one area of agreement among the press was Australia. Because the rumoured location was so far away from everything that was needed to run a research and/or production facility, all agreed it must have to do with nuclear weapons and/or space warfare. Those who went there got nothing of any use except for a couple of newsmen who befriended local aboriginals. However, before they could file their story, they were killed in a road accident on their way back to their hotel near Uluru. The driver of the other car was also killed, and the cause of the accident was never determined. Some called into question whether it was really an accident when there are thousands of miles of nothing in all directions and these two cars happened to be occupying the same road space at the same time. There was not much more on-site investigative journalism after that, and the press retreated to purely speculative journalism.

C&L Corporation

C&L Corporation is a highly successful digital money exchange. In essence, it trades and exchanges different digital money currencies, as well as converting from digital money to hard currency and vice versa. What has made C&L a major cash generator and so successful is its capability for valuing digital money. In essence, digital money can be made to be much more valuable in its digital form provided where you want to spend it accepts payment in digital money. For example, if 100 units of digital currency A could be exchanged for US$20, buying a haircut with hard cash might cost you the whole $20 but if paid in digital currency, it might cost just 50 units of digital currency A – half price.

As they say, 'you can't push coins into a computer terminal'. So, we make use of computer-held accounts accessed using payment cards, credit cards, debit cards, etc. One view argues that your real-world money, dollars and cents, is at risk every time its value is held in a database in the form of your bank balance or an electronic payment account such as a charge card account. Hackers like Rhino will always find a way to divest you of your hard-earned cash by going after your computer-held account. On the other hand, digital money has been purpose-built for the digital/virtual environment with much stronger security controls. So, switch to digital money if you are trading, buying, or selling over the internet. But how unbreakable is digital money? Those dealing in digital money will deny that there has ever been a security breach, while every week we hear of millions of digital currency units being falsely created and put into the accounts of criminals.

The concept of generic or specific purpose virtual currencies has been with us for decades, the so-called barter currencies, the only difference being that now these currencies are fully digital. The above argument favouring digital currencies makes the point that the world is going digital, giving us the Internet, remote working via Teams and Zoom such that we do not need to go out for face-to-face shopping, and we need to pay with electronically held accounts. So why not use digital currencies especially designed for this purpose?

On the question of fraud in digital currencies, it is noted that digital money is identifiable through its serial number and traceable although it can be anonymous. Those peddling digital currencies are at pains to tell you that digital currencies are absolutely safe because they use a security system for moving value called Blockchain. You can find out about it on the Internet if you are interested. Some say that Blockchain is so good that security needs no longer be of concern. However, experience shows that there will always be those setting out to break such systems which they invariably do. As the mantra goes, 'if you do not want your identity or funds stolen, don't go online'.

Even if we accept that digital currencies are secure, useful and convenient, people still will fall for confidence tricks or be persuaded to give out their passwords. Have you had an email saying,

"You are the beneficiary of a long-lost aunt, who has left you $5 million? All you have to do is send £1,000 in digital currency to a numbered digital account to cover storage and legal costs."

You have never heard of the aunt but just in case you send the £1,000. Did you receive the $5 million?

We have to remember what money is and what it should be used for and what it should not be used for. We need money to exchange goods and services for other goods and services. As such it is a promissory note of value universally accepted in terms of something that can be measured, for example: one ounce of pure gold. Money is very useful in that it establishes an agreed trading value and large amounts can be carried in your pocket. But money is just a promissory note and is not a commodity in its own right although it is treated as such. People every day are making fortunes out of trading currencies, lending money, underwriting money and so on. Yet their dealing is doing nothing of real value for the world.

It is in this environment that C&L Corp operates, making billions of real, hard currency dollars, so much so that some were beginning to question what was really going on. Was this a 'mega-Ponzi' that one day will implode? It is particularly noted that great interest in digital currencies has been shown by a number of crime syndicates since here was a possible major new channel for criminal activity. This interest has acted to keep legitimate investors well away as for them the numbers just did not add up if the business was fully legal and so, major crime must be involved. The warning bells were ringing loud and clear.

The world's money men know well who is manipulating hard currencies and they can live with that, but who is doing it on digital currencies? Besides, all currency values can go down as well as up, it is not a one-way street. There is no can't lose scenario even in digital currencies, and although at the moment investors in digital currencies are doing well, with no long-term hard evidence about the currencies, any crash when it comes could well be spectacular.

With these considerations in mind, the clubs of legit traders have collectively shied away from becoming involved in digital currencies and have become determined to highlight its weaknesses and bring their upstart competitors down. SAGE had been invited by C&L Corp to carry out a security audit, especially into the possibility of digital money being falsely created by other than the official banking organisations. SAGE's instructions were clear, find out if they are being ripped off and if so by whom? If a digital currency is at fault, advise C&L so they can take (unspecified) action to kill it.

While he was unsure whether he wanted this business, Chess had two compelling reasons for taking the job; one was money, this was easily his biggest client by turnover, and the second, one of C&L's board members was Sergei Bucholova who was also on the board of STP Industries. Even as an oligarch, there was no way he alone could be funding STP Industries; so there was a strong possibility that there is a connection to C&L and its very long pockets. Chess needed to find out.

For the first time since he started worrying about STP Industries, Chess felt he was getting somewhere. The head of C&L Corp was a recluse known only as Mr Big. No one knew his (or her?) name or had seen him or had even seen a photograph. The speculation was that he had been in an accident, and he (or she) was disfigured. Chess was struck by the similarity between Mr Big and what little he knew of the controller.

General Jim Bray

General Jim Bray's parents lived most of their lives in Idaho, USA. They had a smallholding and were potato farmers. Life was very hard with no certainty year-to-year that the crop would succeed and not be wiped away by disease or the weather. There were some very lean years and young Jim went many a day without eating. It was a surprise to all that Jim grew to be over 6 ft and well built.

For years, two things dominated Jim's mind, to make life easier for his parents and to choose a safe career with no chance of redundancy. He chose the army and enlisted as a private. From that day on, a large proportion of his pay went to his parents until the day that they died. In the desire to make sure he had an ongoing job, did nothing that could lead to his dismissal, Jim was an exemplary soldier, and coupled with his physique he was soon recognised and promoted step by step to Sergeant at which time he applied for and was granted officer training.

His career took off and he was promoted and commended with regularity. Some would say he was in the right place at the right time but in truth, he was good, really good. Making General was the pinnacle of his career, but it was not the highlight. He was no longer soldiering but playing politics. He had saved and invested well during his career and the mantra he had lived by all his adult life of keeping his job was no longer relevant, especially since his parents had died.

He decided to take his army pension and leave as soon as his responsibilities allowed. After this, he could have retired happily but he was an action man and could not sit still. He was approached by many companies seeking to add his name to their letterhead, and he chose one of the larger US-listed companies only to find that it was riddled with politics and mostly about gaining power rather than deploying its products to do good in the world and yes, he accepted that it should do so profitably but not corruptly. He left after three months.

He was attracted by the invitation to join the board of the start-up STP Industries. He liked the prospectus and being in at the start, he judged he could play a large part in making sure its direction remained true to its stated aims. He had no worries about the company's working direction but had other worries, exemplified by the presence of a nasty individual called Vito Serrano.

Tony Silbeck

Rhino made his second mistake, the controller had told him that he could carry on as usual, which was just what he was doing. Unfortunately, he had chosen to target C&L which soon came to Chess's attention via Tam who was monitoring C&L's digital traffic. Under the SAGE – C&L contract, Chess was bound to tell C&L and so, the matter soon came to Mr Big's attention and consequently, it was assumed, to the controller's attention (whether or not they were one and the same person). Although it was true, he had given Silbeck free reign, the controller could not allow the money flow from C&L to be interrupted.

The controller contacted Tony Silbeck with a simple phone call,

"Mr Silbeck, you work for me, the controller. When I rescued you from the clutches of the Spooks, I told you that while you have free reign to do whatever you wish, occasionally I will ask you to take a specific action. This is one such time; you recently started attacking C&L Corp and I want you to stop all activity against them. Those are my instructions." The phone went dead.

Rhino aka Tony Silbeck in STP Industries had his arrogance back. He was fireproof, only ever caught out by the NSA and C&L was not a major government asset, so why stop now? And who is this man who calls himself the controller? Rhino was not about to be beaten by anyone, let alone someone trying scaremongering tactics with no proof (he saw the NSA as being the entity that caught him out and not the controller). So, he decided to continue and be even more overt in his actions regarding C&L Corp. Indeed, he would 'out' the controller.

Within 24 hours, he was in hospital suffering from life-changing inflicted injuries. Serrano does not usually leave his victims alive and capable of continuing their career, but the controller needed Tony Silbeck's special talents. At last, Chess had the proof of a hard linkage between STP Industries and C&L that he needed. And Tony Silbeck would never again go against the controller's orders. But then, there were now many things he would never do again. He wanted revenge very badly, mainly against Serrano but also against the controller who had ordered the attack on him. He knew he had to be careful. If he cleared Serrano's bank accounts, gave him a multi-million-dollar tax bill or substituted Serrano's name for a murderer about to be taken to the electric chair, Serrano would know it was him and he did not want to be hurt again. It would have to be something more physical and not related to Rhino's special skills and Serrano would have to die.

D-Day Minus 2 Years

Up and running for nearly three years, STP Industries now had a staff complement of 700 people, all busy with and excited by their work which they thought was ground-breaking and planet-saving. It was only from the press that the employees found out about the other projects being worked upon. There was no staff movement across projects.

At last, the press had been given some hard information. Products were announced by Michael Kowelski and were immediately available to the world, full-scale production having commenced on all the products being announced:

- Remote sensing cameras and accompanying analytics that are designed for installation in high-flying aircraft, touching space. The camera could penetrate the earth and 'see' 50 centimetres into the ground with a resolution of 20cm. It could discern 90% of the material it was looking at and could be used by prospectors to find gold, opals and diamonds. But it was not made available to the general public, instead, it was sold to research facilities, mining organisations and armies across the world without discrimination and regardless of embargos on trade. This caused much anger and outrage in some countries, but it was soon realised that by making it available in this way, many secret activities would be exposed and the world would be a safer place.

- Wave hopping aeroplanes had been experimented with by the Russians years ago. They had the big advantage of being safe, not far to fall if the engines stopped, and economic. In addition, it was very difficult to see them on the radar, hence the military interest. But the problem that killed their development was the craft's inability to handle large waves and storms. The Russians had had to restrict their tests to inland waterways which were of little use economically. STP Industries had solved the problem and run several trials crossing the Atlantic. They were not in the operating business but helped fund a new company setting up a commercial service operating London to New York in 12 hours of luxury at a price less than a cruise or business class flight and with a carbon footprint an order of magnitude less than either.

- Marlon Whisk had been a pioneer in new battery technology but had not reached a point yet where weight for weight, the battery would take a vehicle further than petrol at the same speed. He had tried several ground-breaking ideas, not afraid of starting again down a different track but not yet succeeded although they had come close on several occasions using different technologies. Then there was the question of charging, mile for mile it still took much longer to charge a battery than to fill a tank with petrol. But STP Industries had done it and had sold the technology to Whisk who had updated his production plant to produce the new battery. There was a massive resurgence in the sales of electric cars, trucks and buses to the benefit of the planet and another win for STP Industries.

Other products not yet in production but rumoured were high-efficiency solar power, a way to break down plastic into harmless chemicals and an efficient means of carbon capture. It was even rumoured that they were working on nuclear fusion and no one any longer doubted that if they were working in this area, they would succeed.

There was no indication about what was going on in Australia despite question after question from the press at these otherwise now informative press conferences.

Peter Larsson

The same advert appeared in selected newspapers across the world, all written in English. It was headed **Pioneers Wanted**.

"Wanted, Pioneers to save the planet. Must be 18-25, fit, able to speak English, educated to high school grade as a minimum and prepared to spend a year away from home out of touch with friends and family. Loving couples encouraged as are specific skills including those trained and training to be doctors, teachers, biologists, carpenters, engineers, psychiatrists and other key skills required for self-sufficiency."

And so, it began!

Peter Larsson is Danish, and at 25, is a trainee medical doctor with one year to go before he would be able to be let loose on the world as a qualified doctor. He likes puzzles and the diagnosis of patient ailments are his best puzzles, which makes him want to be a general practitioner when he completes his studies. On the brink of a career that he loved and felt good about, one would think that he would be happy. It was not that there were no vacant positions in Denmark for young GP's forcing him to apply in the UK where he was quickly taken on with a choice of three locations in the North of England. The real problems were girlfriend trouble and car trouble, both equally prevalent in his mind.

Elsa had been with Peter for 4 years, waiting only for him to qualify before they got married and started the family which she craved. The mere mention of working in the UK had set off a massive argument about how serious he was over their marriage plans.

"If you really love me, I would come before the job." And with that, she gave him back the engagement ring they had chosen together after he proposed, and that was the end of that.

Peter loved his car, his vintage 1962 Volvo P1800, one of the early ones. He had bought the car as a barn find and it was literally a pile of scrap metal. However, he had stripped it right down to its chassis with the body sitting to one side and the engine and gearbox on the other side. He had done all the work himself except for the body respray, in white of course. It had taken him two years in all and now it was used by him as his everyday runabout, turning heads wherever he went. He had had large sums of money offered for the car by collectors, none of which remotely interested him.

Two days after Elsa had given him back the ring, she came to his house to collect her things accompanied by Sven, a handsome youth who was her new boyfriend. Sven wasted no time in telling Peter that they had been seeing each other for several months, two-timing Peter. When they left, it hit him, the engagement was over, they had broken up for real and forever. Peter wanted to be out of the house and away from memories, so he went to see a night-time ice hockey match in a nearby town, some 20 km away.

It was icy out with some snow lightly falling but the Volvo had its winter snow tyres on and Peter had no trouble getting to the match which he saw but did not see. After the match was finished, he could not even tell you who had played, let alone won. He continued his lack of interest in the bar opposite the stadium and would have stayed all night if the barman had not pointed out that the snow was coming down heavily and he had better go if he wanted to get home in one piece. This is precisely what did not happen. He knew not how, where, or when, but he ended up in the hospital and his wrecked car in the police compound.

Back home with his bruises healing, he arranged for the car to be delivered to his home and what he saw brought him to tears. He had run off the road and hit a tree, not full on but a quarter on.

The effect was devastating. The front right suspension had been pushed back and was now under the passenger seat. Worse still, the front right chassis leg was distorted. The whole car would have to be stripped down again, body off, engine out and the chassis straightened.

"Another two years," he moaned aloud although there was nobody near. If it had been a modern car and not a classic car, it would have been written off.

So, one could put it down to him being in a receptive mood when he saw the advert in the paper looking for 'Pioneers'. He wrote to the box number immediately and two weeks later, he was offered a job interview in Helsinki, flights and hotel paid, the interviews to be held at the offices of a company called STP Industries. By then he had started rebuilding his car and had second thoughts about being a pioneer away from home and his beloved car for a year.

He no longer thought a pioneer was in any way right for him. On the other hand, a free trip to Helsinki was not to be sniffed at. So, he accepted knowing full well that if he was offered it, whatever the job was, he would turn it down.

Peter attended the interview and was so disturbed by what he heard about the impending destruction of his world, the opportunity for the pioneers to save the planet, and the obvious need for doctors, that he signed up there and then, even though it was made abundantly clear to him that there was no turning back. Places as pioneers were hot property, even this early, and his training was to start immediately. Peter had become a Pioneer. Most exchanges would be made online but if they had to meet it would be in Helsinki, at the headquarters of STP Industries, a leading benefactor. He was also advised to keep quiet about the pioneers to avoid resentment and inciting mob attacks on the chosen ones.

At the back of his head, warning bells were ringing; why not just stop the destroyer of the earth? Why were the destroyers not seeking out and breaking up the pioneers? Why would they be away for a year? Surely, if the pioneers hide through the destruction of the earth, when they come out all their loved ones would be dead? It just did not add up.

But Peter loved puzzles and here was a big one, in living 3D. He decided to go with the flow and see what it was all about. No matter what they told him, he could always walk away. Now he had better get going on his P1800, hopefully, to complete it before the world is destroyed. At the same time, he also had to put some good hours into his doctoring, you never know, they may be needed.

But the niggles persisted, if the earth was to be destroyed, how would it be done? A nuclear blast would make it unlivable for decades not one year. Create another pandemic using chemical warfare products; unlikely to destroy all humankind and what would it do for all else living on the planet? Make global warming happen quickly and in so doing make the planet unlivable. Again, not in a year. To Peter, the only realistic solution was a nuclear blast, and this would mean living in a bomb-proof, radiation-proof location for decades, which was unthinkable. But so was the alternative – death from the blast. He decided to stick with being a pioneer for the moment, even though in the back of his mind he thought that those behind the pioneers and those planning the destruction of the earth were one and the same; and he would be siding with them.

Julie Oostehuis

Julie Oosterhuis was a white South African, an Afrikaner through and through, believing in the separation of races, white and non-white, lumping all including mixed race into the one non-white camp about which she neither cared nor thought much about. She did not like the way they were treated but put it down to provocation by the non-whites whom she felt were of genetically lower intelligence than her.

But she had to work with them, she was a miner, and all those who carried out the labour-intensive job of mining were non-white, usually African rather than of Indian extract. She was the boss of a specialist team of miners who opened up new seams, dangerous work as there were no supporting timbers in place until they had moved several metres into the new tunnel they were creating.

She was the boss and she made sure they knew it. She believed the fact that they had the fewest accidents of any team was down to her strong management. As a result, her team was fiercely loyal to her and when there was a vacancy, which was not very often, miners queued to join her team.

She worked in the Kloof gold mine which is approximately 60 km southwest of Johannesburg and 20 km from Carletonville, in Mpumalanga Province, South Africa. It was a deep mine, now working at level 46, some 3.3 km below ground.

It had long been reported that uranium was present along with the gold deposits and the company was now also mining uranium as even though gold's price was escalating, uranium was considered more important as a worldwide bargaining item among the major powers as well as the renegade states.

Julie had to learn about radiation and its dangers to protect herself and her team. They all carried indicator tokens which were checked at the start and end of every shift. The problem that they faced all the time was whether they were drilling into a hotspot high concentration of uranium which required them to wear protective clothing and work shorter shifts. But they did not know they had hit a hotspot until they finished their shift and returned to the surface, by which time they could have been exposed for several hours. To counter this problem, Julie insisted everyone in the team checked the indicator token of another team member every hour, even though this was not on the strict policy schedule of the mine's management.

She was married with no children and her husband also worked for the mine, on the surface as a monster dump truck driver; there was no way he would go down the mine. He was boring, uninterested in her, her work, or any other non-work activity, except in the Christian church where he was a lay preacher. Julie found out too late that there was no empathy between them and now they led separate lives, co-existing silently in the same house. She had little interest in the church, and he never asked about her work.

She saw the Pioneer advertisement and was immediately excited, this could be just what she needs to bring her non-work time back to life. She replied to the contact email address given and received a response within an hour. It said they had been overwhelmed by candidates and that she might have been put onto the waiting list ahead of others since she was a miner, but at 30, she was too old. She was disappointed but not to any great extent, she had tried other ways to put the excitement back into her life and there would be more to come, she was certain of that.

Claud Liphook

Claud Liphook's parents were French extract American diplomats spending no more than three years in any one country, including both first world and third world countries, they went where they were told. Their role was to improve the growth and quality of foodstuffs around the world, which being American diplomats, meant those countries of importance and value to the USA. They had spent time in Iraq after their second war and in the UK after Brexit to highlight the variability in their postings.

They worked as a team and their role was to determine the allocation of funding to countries who either had already negotiated agreements for the use of the funding or, as an additional part of the Liphook's role, they would determine both the funding and its allocation. Their son Claud went to many schools and had fill-in private tuition as needed. He was a bright boy and excelled in his academic work, eventually gaining a first at Cambridge University.

The Liphook's job exposed young Claud to the inequities of food availability around the world, the wastage due to poor land and uneducated farming, as well as food mountains going to waste. He also saw the effects of the politicians and captains of industry seeking their own gain over the suffering of others. The grown-up Claud was a kindly well-balanced individual who became an environmentalist. He had inherited a large sum of money when his parents died and was not worried about what the job would pay.

After Cambridge, he joined Greenpeace but once he got to know its long-term plans and had spent a happy year with them he felt his calling to be on a wider front. Making use of his parent's political contacts, he spent another three years touring the world as an environmental consultant working mainly to find funding for needy agricultural causes. Over time, he had been voted onto a number of key Boards and philanthropic organisations which occupied most of his time nowadays. He jumped at the chance to become a founder and director of STP Industries based on its prospectus. He requested the opportunity to invest as a founder but was told that investment was unnecessary as it had all the funding it required, and the shareholding was all taken up by private holdings.

Mr Big

It just did not feel right to Chess, this was not another Facebook, Twitter or Amazon and not even Apple. STP Industries was growing too fast and spending too much. Normally one has an IPO at this point, takes in investor money and everyone gets very rich. But that was not happening here, the company remained private and had not sought funding from anyone. Something that seemed too good to be true, cannot be right.

Chess was particularly worried about Vito Serrano; famous or infamous for being a vicious sadistic bully. He does not care about the law because they are scared of him and keep well away. Chess had once checked up on a rumour that

Serrano had cut off both hands and feet of a local police chief in a remote Idaho town after the policeman had tried to arrest him for badly injuring a man and raping his wife. Chess did not know which came first but he verified the story about the policeman as being true.

Several STP Industries employees were rumoured to be about to leave and talk to the press but went missing and were never seen again. Rumour has it that they moved to the East Coast for a better job, but Tam had searched all the databases, credit card use, tax files, etc and found nothing, not even any close relatives. Knowing Serrano's reputation, Chess warned his people to keep well away and ask no questions.

Rumours about STP industries' activities in Australia were eventually acknowledged by STP Industries as being simply a place where they can carry out research into solar power and extra-terrestrial life. But Chess did not believe a word of it. Why had Professor Wu Lee, a nuclear physicist, disappeared and was rumoured to be in Australia? When Michael Kowelski acknowledged the Australian operation, drones were no longer being shot down but there was little to see, just a couple of nondescript buildings and a very large area of flattened land – billiard table flat. They were no closer to the truth.

The C&L contract with SAGE was to check up on money leaks, both hard currency and virtual. SAGE immediately had a problem which was to separate "genuine" transactions from fake ones. No one knew how to do this or even what was what. This, of course, was the reason SAGE was called in.

It seemed that the C&L CEO was the only one who knew what was going on. C&L was swimming in money, anyone looking at the transaction flow could deduce that and see that only a fraction of it was being shown in its formal reporting. So where was the money going and more importantly, why was SAGE called in?

Everything came back to the mysterious Mr Big. It was clear to Chess that the money was being made in controlling the currency exchange both virtual to virtual and virtual to hard currency. Chess was sure that this mechanism was also being used to 'lose' the excess money, but where was it going? Tam had been working for weeks to try to understand what was going on and had come to only one possible conclusion, somewhere there was a very large money sink. This could be a small country run by a dictator or it could be the only other possibility – STP Industries. It all fitted and answered Chess's long-festering question in terms of HOW but not WHY.

Chess sat down with the Weasel and Tam and debated his beliefs which they all agreed was the only possible solution. He told them that anything to do with C&L's links with STP Industries was top secret and no one must know of their interest in the company. He was, quite frankly, scared of Serrano and told them all he knew about him – now they were scared too. All peripheral activity with reference to STP Industries on this contract was to remain with reference to C&L only.

Chess came to the conclusion that SAGE had been called in to head off questions and official investigations. C&L could validly say they were carrying out a thorough review and that SAGE had been appointed to investigate with a free hand. The press had been rumour-mongering and coming up with all sorts of conspiracy theories, some probably correct. Now with SAGE in place they would have to wait for SAGE's report.

Although this explanation seemed to be the right one, there was a very big hole in it. What happens when SAGE finish their review and reports their findings? Surely this is not what C&L wants – for the money sink to be published. Was something going to happen before SAGE can publish? Has this something to do with STP Industries? Chess was still confused as to why they were called in and clearly, the only way to get an answer was to see Mr Big. But Chess was told by everyone in the company that this was impossible – he sees no one. Yet when asked for a face-to-face interview, Mr Big responded immediately that he would see Chess – alone.

Chess and Jim Bray

Serrano was the enforcer, and very much a hands-on man, although everyone was so scared of him that few now transgressed. The few he had caught spent a minimum of six weeks in hospital with what were called life-changing injuries. As soon as they could, they left town and got as far away as possible. There were some who just disappeared with the rumour put around that they had gone East, but a far more plausible explanation is that they had been killed.

The rules were simple; you did your job and spoke to no one about what you do. You ask no one what they do, and you do not resign although you may be fired with a parting gift from Serrano.

Jim Bray's role was very different, he was the public face of STP Industries security. He supplied the guards, the doorman, crowd control, all the access doors and the sophisticated access control and employee tracking system designed by

Tony Silbeck. He was aware of Serrano's activities and hated it but assumed, rightly, that it would be much worse if Jim's army were not in place. Nevertheless, he promised himself he would deal with Serrano at some point.

Chess had met Jim Bray several times, both in the army and after they had both left. Chess was not surprised when by chance he saw Jim seated in his usual lunch diner. Jim motioned to Chess to join him but as soon as they were together Jim ushered him out the back way to an unmarked grey panel van. Jim remained silent until they had driven 50 miles into the hills and stopped at what had been a barbecue rest area until wildfires had caused them to be banned and the iron barbecues removed. Jim smiled at Chess and was about to apologise for the cloak and dagger approach when Chess smiled back and interrupting Jim said,

"That's exactly what I would have done." They both knew the score.

Jim explained that he took the job as a green field position at the board level to build security and logistics from scratch without interference. He did not know about Serrano until he had started hiring his team and felt he could not then walk away. In any event, perhaps he could control Serrano's excesses, but their meeting place today answered that aim. Serrano was uncontrollable.

Besides his security guard role, Jim also had a logistics role. There were now so many suppliers to STP Industries that he had to manage them including what they said. However, Serrano's reputation had permeated from STP Industries through the supplier community and the same fear Chess determined in those employed by STP Industries had permeated throughout the whole of Silicon Valley. Chess wished it would be different because the inventions had been marvellous and now the Valley was in the grip of fear, and no one could say why such control was necessary.

Chess explained his position, which outwardly was that he did not have one. But when he told Jim about his concerns and what he had found out, Jim was totally onside. They talked at length with Chess only holding back on details of C&L and the link he had found. Jim was similarly quiet about the Australia entity, but Chess put it down to lack of knowledge. Jim also did not know what was going on in Australia.

Eventually, they started talking about what was happening, what STP Industries was doing and why. Chess told Jim his theory, that all these complex projects were put in place to hide another secret project, and the separation of projects and ban on people talking to each other meant that each group could do its bit towards the secret project without knowing what it was. Someone, somewhere will eventually put the whole thing together and make it happen – what? Chess said that he assumed this was what the Australian operation was for which worried him even more because he assumed that Professor Wu Lee was there, and he was a nuclear Physicist. Was someone planning to start a world war?

They drove back in silence and quickly went on their own way as discretely as possible. Nevertheless, Jim was called on by Serrano and reminded of his duties to secrecy – said with friendly words but delivered in a menacing manner. Now they had scratched the surface of STP Industries, but they still did not know what and when, or indeed why. Chess and Jim agreed to keep each other informed and they agreed to meet regularly and openly since they already were friends.

The big question is, who in their right mind would spend billions of dollars on projects simply to hide work on another secret project? The projects completed so far had been wonderful and gone on to make money and bring some good to the world. What one project could be more important than that?

Chess was sure that C&L's missing money was going to STP Industries and every time he put it all together in his mind, he failed to see why SAGE had been called in knowing that SAGE would find the truth and publish it. So, the xxx would hit the fan at some time less than a year hence. Did this mean the secret project would have to be completed by then? And now he had been granted an audience with Mr Big; Chess knew he was being used but how and why? More questions!

Chess turned his attention to the projects that have been delivered and to those rumoured; perhaps he could learn something about the secret project. But first, how had they produced such work in such a short time? They had bought companies where necessary, stripped out what they wanted and then shut them down. They had bought IPR and licences and where they could not, they stole them. In practice, Tony Silbeck had simply hacked into the appropriate government computer and changed the records in favour of STP Industries. Finally, the company bought the best subject matter experts in the world.

Checks and balances, safety and security went by the wayside, the researchers just had to get the job done and money was no object. The actions of STP Industries in killing perfectly good companies and creating major redundancies, the theft of IPR which for some was the value of their life's work, and the shortcut working conditions that other companies were not permitted to adopt, all acted to make STP Industries hated in California, yet they were loved all over the world for the products they delivered.

Chess began to look at what had been produced together with what was rumoured to be in development. Before he put pen to paper, he realised what it was and what was going on. STP Industries were building spacecraft and launching rockets. No wonder the facility in Australia and the levelled ground.

Official product	Use
Remote sensing camera	Survey new planets
Wave hopping plane	Space flight aerodynamics
High efficiency battery	Space flight energy
High efficiency solar power	Space station energy
Carbon capture	Space station health
Plastic breakdown	Space station health
Nuclear fusion (rumoured)	Space flight power; bomb

How many books had been written with this theme? And why such a complex way of doing things? Why not just buy a rocket and a spacecraft and take off from a built site? Why do it all yourself from scratch? It just did not add up, yet everything pointed in this direction. But Chess was no scientist, he would have to find out more.

Ernst Wiegand had a good reputation as a production manager and for this reason, when he started recruiting, all the best production engineers beat a path to his door. Chess had met him but was not on drinking terms with him. Chess also knew Raymond Carver but not in a good way. He had worked in Las Vegas as production director for some major hotel makeovers and was reputed to be ruthless in getting the job done. *Thank goodness,* thought Chess that Ernst is his boss although why would Carver take a number two job; money he supposed?

The production facility had grown quickly, and the newly announced products were rolling off the assembly lines. To any casual observer, all looked good, but a more discerning eye would see a larger capacity than that needed for what was being produced. This was being prepared for the next products to be announced or it could be something else. Again, anyone looking closely would note that a number of the staff were in a different group, working different (and odd) hours. It seemed that Raymond Carver was running this group exclusively while Ernst Wiegand ran the main production shop. This would explain why Carver joined apparently as number 2.

The rumour started and when none of the special group would say a word about what they were doing, the rumours grew and, just as Chess has deduced, it was something to do with space flight and/or satellite technology. The press tried everything to find out – bribery of staff, checking on incoming equipment and raw materials, trying to find hard evidence as to what the Australian operation was all about – all to no avail. And so, the rumours grew into a conspiracy funded by a secret government organisation.

This worried the US government since it was not true but the Russian and Chinese governments could not risk it being true, 'no smoke without fire', and the level of spying on the USA increased dramatically, while diplomatic relations froze, the cold war was back.

Chess was sure now that the intention of the controller was to start a world nuclear war, but he was wrong as he was soon to find out.

Mr Big

Mr Big was not as happy as he might have been. He still produced sufficient excess funds to meet the demands of STP Industries and now they were generating money from their products, and their needs had stabilised. Not only that but 90% of the components they would need to complete their programme had already been bought and paid for. Also, on the side of secrecy, the links between C&L Corp and STP Industries had not been made and the controller had not been linked with Mr Big, except possibly by Chess Chessington and he did not mind that in fact, it would help him in their upcoming discussion.

None of the problems that he might expect worried Mr Big (the controller?); what did worry him were the rumours about spacecraft, satellites, government agency involvement and conspiracy. He did not need the Russians and the Chinese and the US, UK, French and Israeli spooks climbing all over his operation. Thinking of the Russians remined him that Sergei Bucholova knew too much about the links between C&L and STP Industries, he would have to do something about that soon.

Mr Big put aside those thoughts and turned his attention to Chess Chessington. How much did he know? How much would he tell him? Why should he say anything to Chess? It was time, Chess had arrived. Mr Big got ready and then opened the door to Chess. What Chess saw was a person in a black hooded cloak with a full-face mask. It was impossible to tell whether it was a man or woman, black or white. He was greeted by a man's voice with a perfect English accent.

After the usual pleasantries they sat down, and Mr Big started off by asking,

"How much do you know?"

Chess did not expect this but countered by saying,

"I am aware that the large amount of the excess cash you are generating is what is funding STP Industries and that the good, planet-saving products it is making is just a front to hide what it was really doing."

"And what is that?" replied Mr Big.

Chess had the impression that Mr Big was smiling behind the mask, but he could not be sure. Regardless, although worrying for Chess that he might be walking into some sort of trap, he carried on by saying,

"I believe STP Industries are building multiple nuclear weapons and delivery rockets with the intention of starting a world nuclear war."

Mr Big clapped his hands and said, "Very good Chess, may I call you that? But why would I do that, it would destroy most of the world and make the rest uninhabitable for centuries. What plants and animals lived would be damaged by radiation creating a world of monsters." He paused, and continued,

"Of course, we could have discovered another habitable planet and plan to take a chosen few there; or we could just kill all technology, communications, and anything on earth requiring electricity even if just battery power. The world would go back to the stone age and if an 'enlightened' person capable of harnessing the long-dead technology came along, well as they say, 'in the land of the blind, the one-eyed man is king'. Is that not the most likely explanation Chess?"

Chess was dumbfounded, of course, that was the explanation, he needed rockets and space bombs to take out the communications and spy satellite network, and an H-EMP blast alongside cobalt salted nuclear bomb which would kill 90% of all living things on Earth as well as destroy everything with electronic components in them which today, is just about everything.

But why tell him all this? anticipating the question, Mr big continued,

"I see you are wondering why I am telling you all this. I knew you were halfway there and that in time others would arrive at the truth leaving me, C&L Corp, or STP Industries to fight on many fronts. The US government, other country spooks, armed vigilantes, everybody would be after us and there would be no place to hide or complete our task. When you leave here you will go straight to the US president, tell him, no persuade him that this is real, and he must act before it is too late. He will coordinate a single force against us which we believe we can cope with."

Mr Big got up as if to terminate the interview. Chess, seeing the meeting was at an end said,

"Just two more questions, why? And are you the controller?" to which Mr Big responded,

"I am afraid I cannot tell you the answers to those two questions, but you will find out in good time. By the way, you missed the third question which I also would not have answered. When? Goodbye Chess."

Pioneers

There were far too many respondents for the role of pioneer, they wanted a minimum of 10,000 and a maximum of 20,000 to allow for late dropouts; they got 350,000. The selection process was well organised but still tortuous. First, they carried out a paper sift to get the numbers below 100,000. Then they had a series of boot camps around the world, all travel expenses paid for by the organisers. Then they held one-to-one interviews in Helsinki at the STP Industries head office, again all expenses paid. The whole exercise took several months.

What were the candidates told about their mission? They were each told individually and 'privately' that the coronavirus pandemic was not accidental, it was deliberate by forces bent on cleansing the world by destroying humanity except for a hand-picked elite few who would be saved to repopulate the world. No one knows who is doing this, but the next cataclysm is already in train and no one can stop it. It is suspected that they will set off nuclear explosions around the world to destroy everything humankind has built with the radiation making the earth uninhabitable for many years to come.

The pioneer programme aims to play these criminals at their own game. Before the bombs explode, the pioneers will be placed in a deep cave and mine bunkers around the world as well as a group sent to wait in space. Another group, not part of the pioneers will be sent to neutralise the supposed 'elite'. In summary, if – as is likely – this horrendous act comes to pass, then the pioneers will be the ones to save the world. It was made plain to the candidates that their contract was for one year and if the world is still habitable in a year, then their job would be done, and they could go home or be offered a new contract if there was a need. On the other hand, if the world becomes uninhabitable during their initial contracted year, then they would be safe in their caves until it was safe to come out.

The additional carrot was the need to bear children and expand the healthy population as quickly as possible. Sex among the Pioneers was to be encouraged, with as many and varied partners as possible. Most of the candidates bought the story, buoyed by the thought of repopulating the world, as well of course as staying alive. Those perhaps not so gullible were either rejected or chose to leave.

Peter had come to Helsinki for the trip, uncertain as to whether he was going to reject the Pioneer role of hiding out in a cave for years in favour of getting killed instantly when the bomb went off after he had left the Pioneer programme, not an easy choice. On another level, he was attracted by the "sex on tap" story as he had not been near a woman since Elsa left and he was becoming anxious on the sex front. Also, he was a doctor (almost), and they were giving him the hard sell, they wanted him. There was also another issue for him to consider which was the possibility and prospect a new and more virulent and deadly Coronavirus being let loose. The Pioneers would have a chance to remain virus free in their hideaways. They could stay in their bunkers until a vaccine was created. This was the key for Peter who, as a doctor, wanted to help. He committed to becoming a pioneer.

The selected pioneers were told that the period of waiting in the bunkers and in space was predicted to be one year but could be considerably longer if nuclear devices had been set off in which case it could be anything from a few years to a hundred years. For this reason, some of the pioneers would be cryogenically frozen to be re-awakened when the Earth was free to be re-inhabited and the rest would live and have children who would also exit to re-inhabit the world. Pioneers would have the choice of staying awake or sleeping with couples expected to elect to stay awake. There would be some choice between going into a bunker or space so long as the numbers balanced and there was a good spread of skill sets with a bias towards science and research in space.

The pioneers were told that it was expected that they would need to be in place in the bunkers in about a year's time, but it may be sooner, so they must be prepared, and training would start immediately. They should say their goodbyes and meet at the bootcamp locations in one week with nothing more than one knapsack. Money would not be needed.

As predicted, with meticulous attention to detail, Peter, like the other pioneers were called upon in less than a fortnight. They were taken by air to somewhere in central Australia where a new township had been built just for the pioneers. This would be their home and training camp for the next nine months. Singles electing to stay awake were also encouraged to pair off before they entered the bunkers or spaceships. Some with manual and/or technology skills were taken out to help prepare the bunkers together with a separate workforce.

Peter was, once again, beginning to have serious doubts and misgivings. If the training and preparations take about a year and they would be in the bunkers of a minimum of a year, already their commitment to being away from their families has stretched from one year to two years. But his more serious concern was the whole deal. Timing has been defined, major investments were made in the pioneers and their infrastructure, how did they know the timing of the criminal element they were supposed to be guarding against? The Pioneers have made no secret of their plan, why have the criminals not just taken them out? The only rational answer was that those setting up and managing the pioneers and the criminals about to unleash havoc on the Earth were one and the same. But why!

Book 2
Reaction

In South Africa, Julie was worried; the pioneers were real and there was much speculation about their real purpose. The most popular theory was that a rogue nation had acquired the technology to produce a nuclear bomb and that it would use it to start a world nuclear war in which there would be the risk of destruction of the world's entire global population, except for the pioneers who would stay hidden until it was safe to come out and then start to re-populate the world.

To add credence to rumour, governments around the world emphatically denied the rumour or that it was started by their countries. Yet, the US, Russia and China all started their own military exercises and relations were so strained that the press dubbed the times as being the start of a second cold war.

When she told her husband out of genuine concern, he just laughed it off as a scaremongering conspiracy theory given strength by social media. The more she pursued the subject, the angrier he became saying that she was an idiot wife just trying to undermine him and his ability to control his wife. As soon as he said that she let fly with a well-aimed kick at his crotch. It found its mark and he collapsed onto the floor. He was not himself again for two days which he took off work saying he had had a fall. Few believed him but then most just did not care; he was not 'one of the boys' drinking and hoaring week in and week out.

It all came to a head quickly, he moved out and filed for a divorce. They had not been together in the marital sense for some while, so she was not unduly upset, indeed she reasoned that it would give her more unquestioned freedom to do something about her fears. If she could not join the Pioneers she would form her own group of pioneers with a headcount of one.

She knew about radiation from her work, which would help her as she made preparation. She was a miner and clearly, a deep mine would provide the safest place away from radiation and any marauding soldiers or renegades scavenging, raping, and pillaging once the world order had broken down. She had seen all the disaster movies.

She needed a place in the mine where she could store food and vital supplies and hide away. The bottom of the mine would be the furthest from any surface radiation but there were too many people around at that level, besides if there was and nuclear destruction the mine lift would not work, and a 3.5-kilometer climb would be a big problem. She opted for a worked-out disused level about halfway down to allow her easiest access to the lower levels where there was much of the equipment she would need, and deep enough to avoid radiation.

Her one-person pioneer group had now become the main focus of her existence, and she started getting ready for something that might never happen at some unknown time in the future. But the pioneers were real so it must be happening and sometime soon. She began a list of what she would need in her hideaway starting with the location itself. She needed a cavernous location feeding off a tunnel from the main shaft so that her new home could not be spotted without someone physically coming to the right level and going down the right tunnel. Because the level was worked out and disused, many of the tunnels were blocked with a locked door as part of the mine safety regime. She had access to the keys and quite easily found what she wanted; a 300-metre tunnel blocked by a door leading to a closed cavern with no other tunnels leading from it.

The cavern, once mined out, had been used as an equipment store and it was strewn with discarded equipment, mainly broken stuff, but while clearing it all into a corner, she came across some functional items that could be useful to her. Julie began a regular ploy of staying at her place of work after her shift, using her status as a team leader to justify staying to check something or another out. She also took to going down the mine during her off-time. She did not want to arouse suspicion by taking the lift and stopping it at a worked-out level, so would usually take it to the first active level and walk up the escape stairs – just on one km. her friends and co-workers noticed that she was spending more time at the mine which they put down as one effect of the divorce – hiding away and at a loss with what to do with herself. Julie did nothing to dispel this rumour.

Jacob was the longest serving, biggest and strongest of her team and was the natural leader of the work crews. As such, Julie's orders to the men were made via Jacob. But she did not know him and true to her belief, she considered him intellectually inferior to her, so she had never had a conversation with him other than to give him orders. Jacob appeared to be a loner, quiet, never joking with the men and with no stated next of kin (she had checked up on him when he joined her group). He reminded Julie of Big John in the song.

Julie began to notice people looking at her or striking up meaningless conversations; was she being paranoid? She reasoned this must be the case as no one had challenged her and life underground went on as normal. In reality, people were talking about her marriage break-up and the fact that she had no real friends and no outside interests. They reasoned this must be the reason she was spending more time in the mine, her one passion, poor Julie. She also noticed Jacob noticing her, this was not paranoia, it was for sure. What should she do about it? Fortunately, or unfortunately, depending on your view, things were brought to a sudden resolution when Jacob appeared at the door to her new home when she was there making her preparations.

D-Day Minus 1 Year

Professor Wu Lee was indeed in Australia having been shipped there as soon as STP Industries commenced operation and now he was a virtual prisoner as there was nowhere to go outside the facility. He was under enormous pressure and looked haggard and stressed; he was a shadow of his former self.

Construction was moving forward at a great pace, and it looked like 17 separate structures were being built on the flattened area of land by what appeared to be at least five separate companies all racing one another. Although the area being built on was vast and you needed a car to get around the whole site, as far as one could tell from a distance, all constructions appeared to be the same which Prof Lee already knew were to be 17 space rocket launchpads.

Why not just rent launch space on one or more of the now many launchpads around the world? And even if STP Industries wanted to keep everything in-house, why not build just one or two launchpads and send up the rockets and their payloads one after the other? Prof Wu Lee had been kept in the dark about what the intention was, but he was charged with designing and building several types of hydrogen bomb; 2 x 1 megaton H-bombs, 15 x 100 megaton cobalt salted H-bombs and 15 x 20 megaton H-bombs adapted to emit the maximum H-EMP blast. But he was no fool and was beginning to form an informed opinion of what this was all about. 15 bombs to kill all living things and make the planet uninhabitable for 100 years and 15 bombs to generate an H-EMP pulse which will kill all electronics on earth, perhaps a 'belt and braces' approach but just to make sure in case there were any pockets left clear of radiation. So, if this lethal payload is launched by rockets and put into orbit round the planet, the bombs could be exploded simultaneously and the world would be destroyed and every living thing in it.

Even he, the cold-hearted scientist who did not care about the collateral damage he caused so long as he could run his experiments and trials as and when he wanted, shuddered when he thought about it and here, he was, part of the team bringing about the end of everything. This must be wrong he thought, there would be no point to such a move. Perhaps people do not realise what is going to happen; perhaps they think the world will survive ready to be repopulated by a hand-picked group of men and women safely living in a space facility until after the cataclysmic event. But they were wrong in their calculations, and he must let them know. He had tried to do this through his chain of command in the facility but got nowhere, and he fared no better through other routes, once again being fobbed off with platitudes. He was clearly not getting through to the people that count. And so, he continued doing his work and taking the world one step nearer oblivion with every hour he worked.

Jim Bray visited the Australian facility frequently with a contingent of his 'army' with the role of keeping people away. Some journalists more enthusiastic than was good for them had seen too much and had been badly beaten for their troubles and given a warning they would not be so lucky next time. They did not return but others kept trying.

Prof Wu Lee engaged with Jim Bray and told him about his fears. The General thanked him for bringing this to his attention and he promised to deal with it and bring it to the attention of the right people, another platitude. But Jim was shaken by what he had heard, and he believed it. Perhaps Prof Wu Lee had noticed the colour drain from Jim Bray's face. He needed to get back and talk to Chess Chessington PDQ.

There was no sign of any rockets at the facility and Jim Bray had been everywhere in the facility in his job of checking security. There were some massive hangers surrounding the site which could easily house 17 rockets and their payload, but they were empty. He knew from the professor that the payload of bombs was being built here in Australia under the watchful eye of the Wu Lee, who himself was being watched. To move 32 nuclear bombs around the world would be asking for trouble including certain discovery. But the rockets, disassembled were a different case.

Chess had told Jim about the disparity he had detected between the manufacturing capability of the Palo Alto facility and the actual output. Could the production of a self-assembly rocket be what the production facility was doing to fill its capacity? By breaking the rocket into sub-assemblies, the production lines would probably have no clue as to what they were making. Building 17 rockets in Lego form, then shipping the components by various routes and finally assembling them in Australia would all take time – and the hangars were empty. Jim felt a little better knowing there was still time to do something, but what?

Then there were the remote sensing devices being built as part of the set of amazing products developed and being produced, their functionality and design clearly put them in the space industry arena, but STP Industries was not in the space business at least not as yet, and so far with no announcement of the intention to do so. This led to much speculation in the press about space weapons which in turn began to take the shine off this fast-growing, tech industry company. The company made little attempt to scotch the rumours and conspiracy theories, all they said was that this device has powerful military applications not related to space technology and they were in discussions with a number of governments around the world. The rumours grew and are now mainly centred on a space weapon to destroy enemy satellites, and they all agreed that the Australian facility was where the space development was taking place. Even the US Government began to get concerned.

Jim Bray was informed by one of his men in Australia that Professor Wu Lee was in the hospital with life-changing injuries after falling off a hangar roof; no one knew why he was there. Jim should have expected it – Serrano of course. As sad as he was that his meeting with Wu Lee had caused him to 'fall', it did give him some useful information. The design and assembly of the bombs must be complete, but the job is not finished, otherwise, Wu Lee would be dead. Jim assumed he would be needed for the final assembly of the bombs into the rockets. Maybe they could work out a timetable based on how long it would take Wu Lee to recover.

D-Day Minus 9 Months

Chess was all alone in his office working out in his mind how he was to get to the president, past his two staff sentries without telling them what it was about; the president must hear it first. He was just about to make a list of his options and possible opportunities when he was interrupted by a knock on the door. Not his secretary, she does not knock, but she is also his gatekeeper deterring some and announcing others. Then who? Serrano?

He was clearly getting paranoid, it was Jim Bray who immediately grabbed Chess's jacket hanging by the door, pulled Chess and the jacket out of the door and shut it. Jim was also getting paranoid. Chess was about to protest when Jim put his finger to his lips. They went silently to Jim's car and got in, still silently. To Chess's surprise, they drove to the nearest Hertz rental and picked up a small SUV. Only when they had driven away did Jim break the ice.

"You need to hear this," he said, and then recounted all he had found out in Australia. Chess already knew much of it but not total annihilation. They drove on sometimes silent, sometimes arguing. Was Wu Lee wrong, or was he right and whoever was in charge had got his numbers wrong, or was the plan to destroy the world completely and create another Mars? Was this what had happened to Mars?

The discussion then took another turn as they discussed Chess's visit to Mr Big. Chess was sure he was also the controller but could not get him to admit to it. However, it was the subject of their conversation that convinced him. Chess recounted the conversation which told a story very similar to that Jim had related, the only difference being that in Mr Big's version, the world would not be destroyed completely and would be re-populated. Had he said that or had Chess assumed it and not been corrected? Either way, the world was in for a cataclysm if they cannot stop it.

The question that had been on Chess's mind ever since his meeting with Mr Big was why was he told? Mr Big/the controller must know he would try to stop it from happening. They were about 100 miles from the Hertz office when Jim came up with a plausible solution.

"We know that STP Industries is a front to hide the development of the rockets and their payloads, what if there is another level of subterfuge and something else is being built with the rockets as cover?" Chess thought about it and said,

"I think you are right, in which case we are between a rock and a hard place. If we do as we think the controller wants and get the world to attack and shut down STP Industries and destroy the rockets and their payload, if there is another agenda, we will have opened the way for it. On the other hand, if we do nothing and there is no other agenda, we will see the destruction of the world when we might have stopped it."

They agreed that since the rockets had not yet been built and delivered, they had some time in hand and they could consider their options rather than rush in with a knee-jerk reaction. Given this, it was agreed that Jim should do no more for the minute as he was beginning to receive the attention of Serrano. Jim would do his best to stay alive and work at STP Industries watching from the inside. Perhaps he would get a glimpse at the third agenda if there was one.

Chess agreed to hold off talking to the president even though Jim said he could set up a meeting with him. They would hold fire until they were more certain. Chess announced,

"I think I should go to Australia myself to see for myself what is going on. How can we do his without raising suspicion?" Jim responded,

"Why don't I find that information is being leaked out of Ulara and call in the best investigators, SAGE?"

"By that approach," he continued, "there will be no way for any link to be made with C&L Corp even though C&L Corp is among SAGE's clients." Jim thought for a while and then came up with a plausible suggestion. They both agreed but to make sure it was 'Serrano-poof' Jim should rehearse his story.

Jim began,

"I will call SAGE independently as a well-respected security company and ask for their help on the pretext that on my last trip to Australia I uncovered a security leak coming from an internal source. Clearly, I cannot use in-house staff, so I have called in SAGE the well-respected security company with offices in Palo Alto. Of course, I realise how sensitive the site is and the work going on there, so I have insisted that only the SAGE CEO, Chess Chessington works on the job and he goes to Ulara on his own." They both agreed that this approach should stand up and that as well as getting him inside, it should also give him computer access. The obvious downside was that it had to be Chess alone, Tam could not come, and neither could the Weasel. Chess felt the hand of Mr Big somewhere in these arrangements.

As arranged, Chess received an invitation to visit the facility in Ulara to find the leak noted by Jim Bray but not identified. Chess did not travel to Ulara as his first stop, instead, he went to Canberra and met an old friend in the Australian security service, Tom Moore. Tom knew little about STP Industries or the Ulara facility as it is in the Northern Territory and as in the US, power rests in the State, and STP Industries had done nothing illegal.

Tom and Chess agreed to keep each other up to speed on the situation and Tom called his counterpart in Darwin, Sam Tomba, to introduce Chess. Rather nervously for two experienced army men, they both blurted out at the same time,

"Good luck!" and Tom added first, "You will need it, and watch out for Serrano." Chess responded rather weekly but with a smile on his face,

"Nothing to worry about, only the future of humankind in our hands." After they said their goodbyes, Chess took the next flight to Darwin to meet Sam who, perhaps unsurprisingly, turned out to be Aboriginal. Sam knew quite a lot about the facility in Ulara but little about its background and STP Industries. The facility was built on sacred Aboriginal land, something that the controller had not noted and in Australia these days Aboriginal rights are important.

"So how did they get permission to build?" The answer was obvious, bribery, and STP Industries have deep pockets. The offending party had been sacked but by the time the State was ready to instruct STP Industries to remove their development, it had been largely built.

The company had negotiated a deal with the State, to continue operating for a period, then to shut up shop and return the land to its original state as well as make a large donation to the aboriginal community. Chess asked how long the period was and when Sam said there were just nine months left, Chess was horrified and almost sick, the world would end in just nine months! Chess said nothing to Sam about this and quickly recovered himself. Sam said,

"I will instruct my people in Ulara to make contact with you," he stopped without telling him how and when which Chess thought a little odd but put it down to security.

Chess arrived in the Ulara facility at 9 p.m. local time and the place was brightly floodlit but appeared deserted. He was met by a large man, obviously, a security guard who did not bother to introduce himself and simply showed him to his room. Chess was not bothered; he was tired and jet-lagged and was fast asleep in 15 minutes not even bothering to open his suitcase.

He was woken the next morning by a tall American woman clearly on the wrong side of 40 although not unattractive, standing over his bed.

"Good afternoon, Mr Chessington, you have missed our morning but there is no rush. When you are showered and refreshed, find me in my office and I will have a late breakfast ready for you." Before he could answer, she continued,

"By the way, I am the facility manager here, my name is Helen Archibald – they call me Hell because that is the way I run this facility." With that, she turned and left without allowing Chess to respond.

In her office, Hell made sure that Chess was aware of her disapproval of his presence, especially as she had been given orders to allow him full access to systems and locations. To make matters worse, Chess insisted that he be allowed to contact Tam so she can look for faults in their systems and processes.

"Why can't we keep this in-house?" she commented. She had nothing to fear but the role of the whole operation must be kept secret. Reluctantly Hell agreed to Tam having access to systems and processes but without live data.

Chess was relieved, Tam could find the leak, if there really was one, while he explored the facility. Jim Bray had gambled that every computer system used by more than 20 people, will have a leak. In any event, he was in a win-win situation, either Chess finds the leak or Chess proves there is not one. The client should be happy in either case. Chess set up a practical test of the facility, entering and exiting every door and checking that all events were accurately logged. He spent 2 days doing this, asking a few questions in order not to arouse suspicions. But then, Jim Bray had already briefed him. Jim's information was spot on differing only in the large hangars which Jim had found empty but now were full of equipment. Chess could recognise rocket casing but nothing else, it needed an expert's eye. Also, he was rushed out as soon as he had checked the door.

Tam contacted him that night (Australia time) with the leak identified, what was done, how it was done, the name of the perpetrator and the destination of the leak. This was too soon, he needed two more days and asked her to call again with the results in 2 days. That night at about midnight, he felt someone shaking him and he was just about to retaliate when the person shaking him said,

"Sh… I am Sam's man." After 10 minutes, they were in deep but quiet conversation. He was a bush aboriginal who was not an employee and had no right of access. So how did he get in and out without detection? Chess had gone round the whole perimeter and found no security weaknesses. Jonny, that was his name, smiled and Chess promised not to reveal the leak. Jonny asked how he can help,

"Put this memory chip into your phone, go into the big hangars at night and photograph everything that is in them. Then return the memory chip to me." They agreed to meet the same time the following night, but Jonny did not appear.

What had gone wrong? Had he been caught? Was Chess at risk? Just in case he started packing. Then at 3:30 a.m., Jonny turned up, all smiles. He gave the chip to Chess smiled again and was gone. Chess called Tam and transmitted the data on the chip to her. Once she confirmed receipt, he deleted the data on the chip and digitally shredded it.

The next day, he reported Tam's findings to Hell. She thanked him quite genuinely but could not get him out of there quickly enough and made travel arrangements for that same day, routed via Sydney to San Francisco. He thought about changing his route but that might look suspicious. He called Sam and Tom and they both told him not to worry – they were both waiting for him at Sydney airport. He told them little more than he thought they already knew, and he expected that they had copies of the Jonny photographs. He told them about the leak and of the build of rockets with unknown payloads assumed to be nuclear.

When he landed in San Francisco there was a message waiting for him from Sam,

"*The disfigured, dismembered body of the leak had been found.*" Serrano!

D-Day Minus 8 Months

Michael Kowelski was confused and worried. He had no more press releases to present; he had no work to do, and his lines of communication had dried up. He could not even raise anyone via the back channels he had created. In fact, every time he established contact, the person at the other end took a holiday or was reassigned. He was on his own.

What he did glean, mainly from public social media was that the Palo Alto facility was running down with R&D and production moving to Australia. The production of products already on the market would be continued in a slimmed-down Palo Alto facility. His Helsinki head office was also being run down and now only had a skeleton staff. There was no question of firing him or reducing his over-generous pay packet but that did not stop him from worrying; and then there was Serrano!

He wanted to ask questions but did not know who to ask. There was the controller, but Michael had never met him and actually did not know how to contact him. So, he started asking the few people he did know and could contact – starting with Sir James Scott. He turned out to be worse than useless in that he wanted to take the money paid to him as director's fees but keep it as far away from the company as possible. He did not want to become embroiled in what he was sure was some kind of major illegal activity. For this reason, he also asked Michael not to contact him again.

Then he received a message from the controller who seemed to know every action Michael took and every thought in his head,

"STP Industries is going through a period of change and just like the caterpillar, it will emerge as a beautiful butterfly. Please, Michael, hang in there, go to work every day and collect your pay packet every month. As a token of recognition for your good work to date, I am giving you a 10% pay rise," said the controller over the phone in a pleasant but firm voice.

Before Michael could thank the controller, the line went dead, Michael was alone again. He knew he had just received the 'smile nicely but do nothing', the carrot, and as much as he liked money, there had to be a catch. As if to emphasise the point, the stick was soon to come. A package came for him in the next post. It contained photographs, one of Serrano holding aloft a chain saw and a dozen others of different bodies, women as well as men, all horribly mutilated.

Michael knew Serrano and his capabilities, what should he do? He thought the least worst option would be to resign. 24 hours after sending his letter of resignation to all Board members two of Serrano's heavies arrived with a message 'he must not resign' which they made sure he heard by giving him a severe beating, breaking some ribs but leaving his face unmarked. Michael was now hopelessly muddled as well as scared, he had never been involved in violence, white collar crime – yes, but always without violence. The next day he went to the police and asked for protection and, for his own safety he was put in a cell until the police could decide what to do. By the morning he was dead.

Helsinki was shut down. Chess sent his best SAGE field man, the Weasel, to nose around but he came up with nothing except a mention of the name, the controller.

Julie and Jacob

For the first time since Julie had recruited Jacob onto her team, he spoke without being asked or otherwise prompted,

"What you doing boss? I thought you were stealing but now I see all this, I don't think so. Are you setting up your own private mining operation? If so, how do you get the goods out? I don't want no trouble so I will leave your team."

Julie's head was throbbing, she had never had so much pressure requiring instant resolution, giving the wrong answer and her enterprise was at an end, most likely as well as her job. Meanwhile, Jacob was waiting. But She was the boss and Jacob did what he was told without question. She made her mind up, she would bluff it out and tell him where to go, after all, who would believe him against Julie, and would he risk his job? Before she could get the words out, he started to move and she crumbled blurting out the first thing that came into her head,

"Stop, it is not what you think," Was she going to confide in this lower intelligence black giant whom she had always despised along with the rest of his race. But then she recovered her composure and knew she could control him just like normal and he would do as he was told without telling the rest of his crew.

Julie had had a shock the previous evening after work when she was going on her usual drive out of town, away from the mine and into the countryside, always finding something new. She just loved this country, her country. She came across what seemed at first glance to be the entrance to a mine, but it was in the wrong place, sited at the base of a small mountain or large hill. People were busy around the entrance, mainly moving crates and other goods through giant steel doors and into the tunnel beyond; she could see no more.

There was no hint of secrecy and the group of people working seemed happy in their jobs, working together regardless of colour. She realised that this was a Pioneer's retreat or future home. The tunnel must go deep into the mountain and would certainly provide protection for the inhabitants from explosion and radiation. She also realised that this must not be the only bunker and that others must be sited in similar places around the world. She felt scared, excited, the need to rush back to complete her safety home in the mine, and an overwhelming desire to stop, shut her eyes and think, taking it all in. This is real. It is really going to happen!

But she did not know what. The rumour mills had everything from an extra-terrestrial invasion to full-scale nuclear war. Nevertheless, she felt vindicated in her actions, she was on the right track. She would come back frequently to see what was going on, mainly to see when they are ready which will give her a clue as to when the event will happen.

She said to Jacob,

"The world is going to end, there will be a nuclear war and the population of the world will be wiped out by bombing and radiation. There are some called pioneers who have been selected to hide in bunkers to come out when it is all over and repopulate the world. At least that is what people believe." To her surprise, Jacob responded,

"Yes, I have read about that and thought of preparing a safe hideaway but then I realised that this must be about getting rid of the blacks and creating an all-white world. So, I did nothing and am waiting for the end."

Julie was shocked, he was clearly literate, had some intelligence and viewed apartheid from a diametrically opposite standpoint to her. He believed in racial separation but in a black world. She remembered what she had seen in the bunker, mixed races working and living together not her 'cup of tea', but it showed that Jacob was clearly wrong about it being a black purge.

Julie decided she had no choice; she had to overcome her lifelong beliefs and try to work with this man. She told Jacob of her plans and actions to date and hoped he would at least not tell on her and at best, help her, she needed muscle to move heavy equipment into her new home to be. There was a subtle change in their relationship, she was no longer talking down to him. She would have to watch that back on the team and treat him in her normal manner.

Up to this point, both of them had assumed that this home would be for just Julie and Jacob would have to fend for himself and nothing was said about it. Jacob went only as far as to say,

"I will help you boss and do as you say. I will not tell on you." She decided that she still could not trust him, her lifelong beliefs holding her back. Perhaps she could cement his loyalty by proving this was real.

"Jacob," she continued, "Have you heard about the pioneers." And somewhat to her surprise, he nodded,

"Yes, boss." She told him about the bunker she had found and offered to take him there to prove it was really happening. There was an obvious difficulty with this plan, she could not be seen driving Jacob in her car. He had to make his own way to the edge of the town and away from the mine. She would meet him there and take him on to the bunker.

What he saw when he got there made him open his eyes wide with incredulity. He looked closely at what was happening and realised the pioneers were planning for a long stay. On the way back, before she dropped him off, Julie said,

"If you help me, I will help you create a space for you to live in during the bombing until it is all over. We will have separate areas, locked off from one another but sharing facilities such as power generation. What do you think? Will I be able to trust you?"

Jacob did not answer. Did he want to survive with the same domineering boss when this is all over? Did he really want to live through and beyond the event? Will he run too great a risk of being caught and thrown into prison?

"Can I trust you?" he asked, "if we come out the other end, I want to live like those we saw at the bunker, all races combining happily. I don't want you to be my boss woman any longer." Shocks were coming thick and fast to Julie. Now this black man was setting conditions on her. But she knew that their chances of survival were low and even if they survived the onslaught, it would be a long time before they could come out into the 'new' world. So, what the heck,

"I agree, and you can trust me."

Claud Liphook

Claud Liphook was not your average tree hugger. He was well dressed, charming and did not decry the opposition, instead, he tried to win the argument using logic and hard facts. And he was winning, he was well thought of by governments across the world; he was on numerous committees and had his name on strategy papers produced in 37 languages.

He agreed to serve as a founder Board member for STP Industries based on what he was told by Michael Kowelski as well as positive rumours milling around the business community, although no-one knew the source of these rumours.

So far, he had not been disappointed, valuable, climate-supporting products had been developed and delivered, for example, better battery technology had boosted the electric vehicle market such that four out of five new trucks were electric, almost up with the motor car conversion.

Chess and Claud had known each other for some time and had become quite good friends although their extensive travels, especially Claud's globetrotting activities, meant that they were rarely able to get together. However, today Chess made sure that he and Claud met face-to-face the next time Claud was in the country. Chess said he would fly to meet Claud wherever he landed, so much so that Claud began to get a bad feeling in his stomach, Chess was not a knee-jerk person.

They met in Las Vegas of all places; Claud was chairing a conference there. After a pleasant meal during which nothing contentious was discussed, Chess steered Claud to the hotel car park where he ushered him into a rental, and they drove off into the desert – the same procedure Jim Bray had used with Chess. They stopped about 50 miles out of town and Chess related the whole story to Claud, at least as far as he knew it. To say Claud was shocked was putting it mildly, he had been totally hoodwinked and his name used to cover up an impending world disaster. He had even been awarded the STP Industries Golden Globe 2 years running.

They debated what was really going on, a hidden agenda behind the company's overt activities, and now possibly a third agenda hidden behind those two.

"I will resign immediately and go public on a worldwide stage. I cannot have the Liphook name associated with this" Claud almost screamed, but Chess counselled against that. Firstly, he would almost certainly be killed by Serrano, secondly, if he stayed, he would be able to act as a conduit to Chess. And thirdly, they needed to know for sure whether there is a third agenda and if so, what it is about.

"OK," said Claud, "but I want to distance myself as far as I can from STP Industries, its buildings and its people. I think a world tour is called for, one in which I can look for signs of anything unusual. After all, this is supposed to be a global event." Claud went on to say that he would start in Australia where he had good government friends as well as a number of aboriginal friends including some working in the Uluru area for the security forces under Sam Tomba. Chess was delighted and related his own dealings with Sam and his boys.

Chess knew that STP Industries had eyes and ears everywhere, which was why he had booked a rental and driven them into the desert. Claud took note but had already deduced the way things were going to go for him over the coming months. He thanked goodness for his earlier explorer life where he had encountered all sorts of adversity and managed to overcome them.

Shaun Murphy

Shaun Murphy is an Irish American born in New Jersey of Irish Immigrants some 40 years ago. At 5ft 6ins, he was not big but was very stocky and had more than held his own in many a fist fight. He was an experienced manual worker in the tunnelling industry. Today he is working in Albuquerque, New Mexico, working on the construction of a 5-mile tunnel for a new light rail system. In recent years, business in Albuquerque had outgrown the transport infrastructure which was racing to catch up.

Shaun is one of the more experienced men on the project and after his colleagues had broken through three weeks ago, he was tasked with installing the ventilation system, a precursor for allowing other crews in to fit out the tunnel. There were just three of them, all wearing masks to filter out the dust and the stale air, near the centre of the tunnel they were forced to don oxygen cylinders and breathe oxygen, so bad was the air. The tunnellers had their own air supply as part of the tunnelling equipment but now that they had gone and taken the tunnelling equipment with them, reliance was on the three of them to instal the permanent ventilation system. Their estimated time to completion, testing and shakedown was six months. The time was critical as no one else could work in the tunnel until this job was completed although the workforce would remain busy doing other work on the project.

He was not interested in politics or the news, so long as it did not directly affect him. All he wanted was to do his work, earn his money and drink with his friends. Despite the press being full of WW3, alien invasion and the destruction of the earth, he took no notice of it in and carried on his life as usual. His marriage had broken down fairly soon after the wedding as a result of his Friday night absences, coming back on Saturday the worse for wear, often bruised and still drunk and most times with the scent of a woman on him. But he never physically abused his wife and kept paying her a reasonable sum every week.

Validation

Was there really a third agenda? If not, what was the aim, 'destroy the planet and all living things on it?' why? There had to be another agenda and it had to be at another location, a secret fourth location.

Claud said he would take the opportunity of his already planned world tour to see if he could find the fourth location as well as alert other governments and security organisations, always noting that the controller had ears everywhere.

Claud tried to triangulate the known STP Industries locations to find the closest location to the three known locations for no good reason except he had no other clue as to where he should look. He came up with Libya, not his favourite place and unlikely to commit to the controller as he would wish, especially as there appears to be no one government in charge. However, this is where he would start. He had no good government contacts, and, in any event, he did not wish to be seen siding with one group over another, and there was no way he would have anything to do with the Libyan security services, so he decided to make contact with a university there.

An ex-colleague of Claud's from his days at Cambridge University now had the natural sciences chair at Misurata University in Libya and he thought this would be a good starting point. Thank goodness for the Cambridge University Alumni network – he could find a friend almost anywhere in the world. Ben Jelly, as he was known to the English, welcomed Claud with open arms and had arranged a full educational and social programme for him which he accepted gratefully knowing this would provide him with the cover he needed to hide his real purpose in coming.

When Claud and Ben had some time alone together, Claud wove a cover story that was not far from the truth. He explained that he was looking at Domesday scenarios in case the world climate change reached its critical point and life could no longer be sustained. Part of the task was to seek out the mountain and underground caves where people could live for years or centuries. One of the possible locations identified was in Libya. It had been decided to create separate teams to locate, test and prove locations. Claud's group were identifying the number and general locations needed to ensure the survival of some regardless of whether it became too hot, too cold, too wet, or too dry. Another team would identify specific sites and fit them out while a third team set up a living trial.

It was of course essential that there is absolute secrecy about arrangements for a Domesday scenario. If word got out, public panic would break out and all the bunkers would be attacked and destroyed. Claud had not been told where the sites were and he now had to find the sites, report on how easy this was, and find out how secure they were. In the best scenario, he would not be able to find any.

Ben was amazed and had clearly bought the whole story. After he calmed down and they exchanged 'gosh' and 'wow' words, Ben said,

"This might explain something odd that is going on which most people have put down to being another armed faction, but they are not acting like one, no firing of guns into the air, no armoured cars and so on." He went on to explain that in the Tibesti mountains in the south of Libya, groups of men and women had arrived over a three month period. Totally self-sufficient they had brought their own food, erected their own buildings and tents, brought in heavy equipment and started mining. But there is nothing there to mine!

Ben had not been to see them himself but some of his colleagues had.

"Apparently," said Ben, "the story is that they are mining but would not say what they were digging for. And, when the government arrived to charge them taxes based on what they were extracting, again they refused to say and consequently paid the highest rate of tax without complaint. Also, now they have dug their way into the marvellous caves in the Tibesti mountains, they have moved everything inside, mounted heavy steel doors on the entrance which are closed at night but without being aggressive in any way to deter visitors." He went on,

"Estimates others have made is that there must be about 1,000 people there although now everything is inside the site and it generally looks deserted. And one final point," he added,

"There appears to be an unusually high percentage of women in the group, over 50% I am told."

Claud knew this was it, he had found a bunker, but 1,000 people meant this is a serious venture. Who were they, and where did they come from? He must tell Chess immediately, and there would be no point going to the site if all he could see would be a pair of steel doors covering an entrance.

Claud told Ben that it was exactly what he was looking for and it appears to be very well structured and organised. Claud tried hard to suppress his amazement that there was already a population of 1,000 people living there. But Ben said nothing more.

It was now abundantly clear there was a third agenda.

D-Day Minus 6 Months

Even though he was scared of Serrano, Claud felt he was too high profile on a world stage for Serrano to kill him, a least not yet; and since the controller clearly had a role for Jim Bray and Chess as unknowing pawns in a global chess game, Claud assumed that he was also being used, implying the controller would stop Serrano going against any of the three of them. Claud tendered his resignation from the Board of STP Industries and he was pleasantly surprised to find he was still alive the next morning.

Chess had given his RV a thorough security sweep and installed a powerful jamming device and the three of them were now parked in the RV in the car park of the Venetian Resort hotel in Las Vegas, in plain sight. This was thought to be the best hiding place, especially since the place was always crowded which would make it difficult for anyone to launch a street attack. And there were at least 19 other RVs in the car park.

The first item on their agenda was organisation. They needed somewhere secure where they could talk and store documents and evidence. Chess was the obvious person to handle this and without saying a word, fired up the RV, nosed out of the car park into traffic and headed out of town. He said,

"Let's stay near Las Vegas for all the reasons we have previously discussed, but let's find somewhere more secluded for our command post."

They drove about 30 miles to Boulder City and found a commercial property realtor. He had a new, windowless secure warehouse on his books which he was most anxious to dispose of. It had been purpose-built as a secure, 'cloud backup data centre' specifically for a company that unfortunately had been bought out just as the building had been completed and the new owners had walked away from the deal. For Chess and Claud, it was ideal with good communications, cable ducting throughout, standby power supply and strong physical security.

Chess asked, "Can we carry out some building work to improve security?" To which realtor, surprised that anyone would want even more security than the purpose-built building already had accepted without qualification,

"Of course," he almost shouted. He was so pleased to have a client for the building which he thought he would be stuck with for months if not years, that he would agree to almost anything. They signed a two-year lease, and left the keys with the realtor saying their people would be along to take possession in a day or so; then they left.

Chess told the others he would get his people to fit out the building over the coming two weeks.

They made their now usual drive into the desert, parked and started talking about the situation, Claud reported on the Libya facility, and they were all in a state of shock when Claud reported that the facility was complete or nearly so, and already populated with about 1,000 people. Claud confirmed the number was about 1,000 and not 10, or 100 or even one million. The third agenda exists, and Armageddon can only be a matter of months away.

Worse news was to come, Claud had put out feelers and he had been informed of up to 18 more possible bunkers spread around the world, some uncertain, others for sure. He intended to go back onto his world tour and check up on all of them. He would start with one near Adelaide as soon as they had made their plans.

Their immediate plan was to get their HQ up and running, plan their information-gathering strategy and decide who to call and when. They must inform the US President, but they cannot yet as they do not know which agenda is the right one, what to recommend and when. What they had learned that day was that there is definitely a third agenda but given that, there are a number of possible scenarios:

- The third agenda is a red herring, and the plan always was to destroy the Earth with no survivors. Under this scenario, it would be possible for an elite, chosen few to colonise another planet if a suitable one could be found
- The third agenda is real, everyone on Earth is killed except those in the bunkers. After a suitable time, those in the bunkers would emerge and repopulate the world
- Nothing happens, this is a complex scheme to hold the world to ransom
- Precipitate World War 3 by selectively bombing the US, Russia and China
- Other scenarios are a combination of the above.

None of them could hazard an educated guess as to what was afoot. So, telling the President would be pointless at this time even if they were believed.

Once back at SAGE, Chess instructed the Weasel and Tam to fit out the building they had rented. All communications to be encrypted with better than 128-bit public key data encryption and with them managing their own master key. This would provide service to just the three of them and Jim would have to square that away with the NSA which wants access to everything. The building must act as an unattended switching centre for voice and data so that any one of them could communicate with any other securely, wherever they were in the world.

Communications with others outside the three of them would use best-of-breed, normal security techniques. Finally, the building was to be booby-trapped to explode and be razed to the ground from a signal sent by any of them wherever they were and without regard to anyone being in the building at that time. The whole building perimeter to be secured with internet-based CCTV and intelligent door locks. All doors to be replaced with heavy gauge, double skin, steel doors filled with insulation to negate the heat from a thermal lance.

D-Day Minus 4 Months

Chess's team had completed the upgrade to the building in Boulder City and fully kitted it out all in the space of one month. They now had a secure location to work from but more crucially, they were able to communicate securely with one another no matter where they were in the world. The NSA, as expected, had kicked up a fuss but Jim Bray had resolved that with help he assumed, from the controller.

They were sure now that there was a third agenda and that it was of vast scale and complexity with probably more than 20,000 people involved. The project must have been started about the same time as STP Industries was founded, and the cost on top of the cost of STP Industries' overt and hidden activities would certainly eclipse the GDP of several small countries. This was even more than C&L could provide and Chess made a note to investigate this angle as soon as possible.

They had spent many hours debating the subject, with Claud calling in from wherever he was in the world, but they still had a number of key unknowns that had to be answered before they could take this to the President or go public:

- The main question WHY, what is the purpose of the plan?
- How does the second agenda fit with the third agenda?
- How do you kill everyone on Earth without making the Earth uninhabitable for those in the bunkers?
- How were those in the bunkers selected?
- What are the plans for the post-apocalypse time?
- Is it all a hoax?

They spent more time looking at the possible reason for having both agendas two and three especially as it left the whole project twice as open for discovery compared with just one secret project. Then they hit on the obvious answer – the controller was hedging his bets. The scenario would be something like this:

82

- Agenda 2
- Send up rockets with a satellite in each plus a complement of new world volunteers
- Deploy the satellites around the world in a circulating in a low orbit
- Satellite payloads contain nuclear bombs, probably Cobalt impregnated and set up to provide a strong EMR pulse to kill all the devices of the modern world
- Rockets continue on taking the volunteers to a new world or to a place to wait for the Earth to become habitable once again and repopulate it
- Agenda 3
- There were, as far as they could tell, about 19 or probably 20 bunkers in caves within mountains or at the bottom of deep mines
- Each seemed to be able to hold and house between 500 and 1,000 men and women and keep them alive and in the bunker, for however long it took the Earth to recover and radiation levels to reduce significantly. This could be 100 years!
- Then they would emerge and repopulate the Earth
- The Hedge
- The Earth could be destroyed and break up in which case those in the rockets would seek a new home
- Killing all on Earth will also kill all those in the bunkers in which case those in the rockets would seek a new home
- It would take too long for the Earth to become habitable again and those in the bunkers would die out in which case those in the rockets would seek a new home
- It takes too long for those in the rockets to find a new home and they die out in which case the survival of those in the bunkers becomes paramount
- The new planet for the space travellers proves hostile and they are all killed
- If a new planet is not identified before departure, plan B comes into play. The rocket population takes with them all the tools and equipment needed to join the rockets together and convert them into a space station. They would live on it until the Earth once again became habitable. Of course, they would have to be able to recover the space station into rockets, so they could travel back to Earth.

83

Although they may be wrong in detail, each knew this was what was to happen. It was a very risky but great plan, its only downside was that it meant killing most of the world's population, billions of people – and they had become inadvertently part of it.

So, what do they do now? They would become a laughingstock if they went public with this, and the controller would no longer need them; so, Serrano would ensure they would all soon be dead. It was Claud who came up with a solution.

"Sam Tomba, whom I know well is in the Australian security service and already knows enough of the story to believe something big is happening. Let's use Sam as a conduit to the top of the Australian security service and from there to the Australian Government and the rest of the world leaders. It will be up to them to decide if, when and how to go public."

D-Day Minus 3 Months

Of course, the story leaks out with many inaccuracies, accusations of conspiracies, governments being held to account and the usual countries accusing each other of manufacturing what was clearly a nonsense story as a cover for what was really being planned. Nevertheless, the clear theme running through all the stories was that of country A attacking country B with country C opportunistically taking advantage. Who are A, B and C – to coin a phrase, 'the usual suspects.' The only unknown was which country adopts which role.

And it seemed to be working, tensions were ratcheting up with no 'sensible' mediator, just a growing angry population in countries across the world being egged on by unseen forces. Not to be left out, a number of mid-East countries tried to seize the advantage by declaring war on their local enemy, expecting their big power ally to intervene. But that did not happen, they were too busy facing off against one another leaving the mid-East warmongers to go it alone or back down. What actually happened was a great surprise to everyone, surely this country had thought it through? A small nuclear bomb exploded too near its border, and half the aggressor's country became an uninhabitable radiation zone. The target of the aggression, although equally radiation damaged in part, just did nothing, they were not so stupid as to also shoot themselves in the foot and make their whole country as well as half the surrounding region uninhabitable. Eventually, all realised there was a third force in play, trying to stir up trouble. The arguments died down but not for long.

In the ensuing weeks, several countries found nuclear devices hidden in their busiest locations such as New York's Times Square. So, the accusations continued, although the more pragmatic realised that the devices were found too easily, and none had exploded. This was clearly an exercise in stirring up more trouble, so much so that the world leaders began to fear that control would be taken out of their hands by a group of hotheads who would start WW3 themselves. Perhaps this was the aim all along, to create a situation leading to world destruction by the people themselves. But if that was true, why were satellites, nuclear bombs, and space rockets being produced?

In the end, common sense prevailed, and the major powers got together, agreed they were being set up and vowed to work together to find the *agent provocateur*. The US Government took action and arrested most of STP Industries senior managers and shut down all the STP Industries buildings in California. There were no complaints from anyone in California, whether or not they worked for STP Industries. The smile came back to everyone's face.

The only bad effect was to send Serrano off the rails if he was not there already, sending him on a killing and torturing spree in an attempt to stop ex-employees talking. Like most everyone else, Jim Bray had had enough and declared,

"I feel responsible for allowing Serrano to continue for so long sadistically killing and maiming in the name of the company in which I am a director. It is time I sorted this out once and for all." He assembled his whole 'army' for a showdown with Serrano who revelled at the idea. He and his thugs would show the general who was the top dog.

But Serrano was too arrogant and thought himself untouchable. He approached the coming battle in the same way as the British army Light Brigade charging the French so many years ago. He was all attack, no defence and no strategy. They were armed with knives, machetes and cudgels for their favourite hand-to-hand fighting. Jim, on the other hand, did not want to risk his men, all he wanted was to just win. He armed his men with semi-automatic guns deployed them out of sight and waited, just like the Light Brigade again, only this time we are on the side of the French. Serrano and his men burst into the trap. It was a slaughter, not one of Serrano's men got through to fight hand to hand. Within 10 minutes all were dead but there was no sign of Serrano.

Jim did not revel in the wholesale slaughter, but he knew it had to be done, and not finding Serrano worried him deeply. For the first time in a very long time, he was scared. What would that madman do now – to him! He had better get Serrano attended to ASAP, but how? Serrano would be after him and would choose the time and place to suit himself. Jim was scared, very scared.

But he need not have worried, another party was taking pleasure in dealing with Serrano. Rhino knew of the impending showdown between the armies of Jim Bray and Serrano and decided it was time at last to exact his revenge. Just before the opening attack, Serrano had received an anonymous message that

Silbeck was using the distraction of the upcoming battle to attack his bank accounts. He went back to the gang's warehouse headquarters and started to examine what Silbeck had done. He was revelling in the thought of what he would do to him once his people had won the battle against Jim Bray's men when the fire alarm rang.

"Strange," thought Serrano, "I don't smell burning." Serrano suddenly realized that it was a trap, here he was on his own in the building with no armed guards. Quite correctly, the sprinklers came on and for an instant, Serrano smiled at what he was going to do to Silbeck but then, the sprinklers reached him and his smile turned into abject pain. Wherever he went, whatever he did, it continued to rain Sulphuric down on him. His clothes had dissolved and most of his skin too and now it had reached his bones. The sprinklers stopped as quickly as they h ad started, and a rubber-suited man appeared at the door. It was Tony Silbeck. Serrano looked at him with pleading eyes, the acid not having done its work there yet. Tony said,

"I could let you live in pain and deformity for the rest of your life, but that is not good enough for me." And with that, he took the shotgun dangling under his right shoulder and shot his balls off. Serrano could not have screamed any louder. Rhino turned and left the building locking the door behind him. Serrano was found the next day, or the tangled mess of bone and flesh that was left, however, Jim waited cautiously for DNA proof and when it came, he was visibly relieved. No one owned up to doing the deed and there were many names in the hat, but no one tried very hard to identify them.

Doubts

During this period, Julie and Jacob each began to have doubts; what was he doing consorting with a white supremacist, and what was she doing with an inferior black? Nevertheless, without realising it, each was softening their attitude towards the other. But that was not their only doubt, was it really going to happen? Were they wasting their time? They had both tracked the goings-on in the world and the latest assurances given by world leaders, but the Pioneers were still there and who would invest so much money in the construction of a bunker as well as supporting all those Pioneers, they had worked out there were about 1,000 in this bunker alone? They both concluded they were doing the right thing.

Meanwhile, Peter's doubts had returned. He knew that just one year locked down in the bunker was not on if there really was going to be a worldwide nuclear holocaust, but he could not countenance a stay of decades in the bunker. So, was it all a fake with the idea of attempting to blackmail the world? Then there were the cryogenic coffins, not cheap even if they are fakes just for show. He genuinely believed they would be there for decades. What should he do? He truly wished he could turn the clock back and this time not apply to the pioneers, even though this would mean him dying when the bombs came. At least that way he would not know what was about to happen. But he did know, and he really had no choice but to stay.

The possibility of WW3 and/or the destruction of earth were people's main topics of conversation, including Shaun's friends when they got together, but Shaun was having none of it. His life centred around work, drinking and women, and overall working hard so he could earn enough to have a good time. If it was to happen, then it would happen and they would all be dead, there was no use worrying about something you could do nothing about. In the meantime, he had a lifestyle to maintain and a life to enjoy.

The coming together of the major powers to fight an unknown enemy was a unique event, never before had this happened. We had had the League of Nations after the first world war which failed and now have the United Nations, but these are clearly talking shops with countries posturing for recognition, power, and most of all, vetoing decisions they do not agree with, the result being that very few multinational decisions are made. The UN was clearly not the right place for the group of major powers to work to save the world.

The group met secretly, without fuss or self-promotion and got down to work. They needed to know the WHO if they were to stop the third party's action to destroy the world but first, they discussed the WHY. The obvious contenders were, nationalism leading to a cold war, religion spurred on by fundamentalists, economic rivalry controlled by the leaders of the multinationals, and the power in the hands of those at the meeting.

All these were discounted as not having a reason to start WW3 or destroy the world except for the issue of power and those in the room had to either trust each other or give up before they started. They agreed to trust each other, each making a formal declaration to the others, some enthusiastically, others less so, but in the end, they started their work united in purpose.

Via their security services and the recent events of the bomb hoax, they knew of the efforts of Chess, Jim and Claud and called them in for a briefing which they gladly accepted and were able to tell the whole story as far as they knew it to the world's key players. It was a major step forward for them and they agreed to maintain an open channel between them all. Chess, however, raised the point that the controller seemed to have eyes and ears everywhere, so they must be very careful in their meetings and discussions.

Chess was visibly relieved, at last, there was light at the end of the tunnel. The world powers were together, STP Industries was no more, Serrano was dead, and they knew quite a lot, but not enough, about the Australian facility.

Book 3
Endgame

D-Day Minus 60 Days

There was a universal sigh of relief at STP Industries' demise, and its hidden agenda foiled. The Helsinki facility had been shut down when Michael Kowelski died and now the California buildings were being dismantled. Chess got in before the wreckers started their demolition work to see if he could find any evidence of agenda 2 or agenda 3 development and build. But either he was too late, or the equipment build had gone elsewhere.

Now that Serrano was dead, the ex-staff were much more ready to talk. However, it turned out that Chess knew more than any of them. The only area of interest to him came from the nuclear fusion development team. Professor Wu Lee had sent them plans for a stable and controllable Nuclear Fusion system that would revolutionise power generation across the world. Here was the holy grail that would eclipse everything else STP industries was working on. Strangely, and for no good reason that anyone would or could explain, it was mothballed and instead they were put to work on nuclear fission – bombs. In addition, they had a separate sub-project which was to study high-altitude electromagnetic pulses (H-EMP). The picture was becoming clearer.

But not everything in the garden was rosy, the bunkers were there, manned and sealed and with the inhabitants clearly expecting something to happen in the near or very near future. Then, without any prior notification, 1,000 people turned up in Australia at the Ulara facility and were promptly allowed in and not seen again.

It was apparent that things were nearly in place for the event to start, and Chess' men were back re-examining the California facilities, which had not yielded anything useful so far and even though Chess knew that the command-and-control centre of all the complex of systems being assembled was not there, they had to go through the motions. It had to be somewhere away from the launch site and until Chess found it and shut it down, the danger remained. He called Claud and they arranged to meet in Helsinki, together with the Weasel and Tam. After a week of forensic searching, they confirmed what they already knew, the command-and-control centre was not in Helsinki, and it was not in STP Industries old location in Palo Alto. What now?

D-Day Minus 45 Days

Claud carried on his world tour, now concentrating on identifying the bunkers and finding out as much as he could about them, which was precious little, and although they had by now identified 19 bunkers pretty evenly spread around the world leading them to assume they must have found all the bunkers, on second thoughts they realised no-one would install 19, so they revised their assumptions and agreed they had missed one. Whether or not they could easily break down a bunker entrance door was uncertain, however, it would in any event compromise the bunker and if the worst happens, they would be accountable for the deaths of 1,000 people. They chose to leave the bunkers alone making no contact with the pioneers.

What they could do in some cases, was to monitor any late goods going in which was precious little. But they could tie it in with the description of goods and photographs supplied by Ben Jelly. Most of the goods were comprised of scientific equipment and the tools one would expect. Then there was food production equipment, and finally, the unknown packages. Claud thought he recognised some operating theatre equipment but could not tell its exact purpose. They would have to infiltrate a bunker to get more, and they did not want to do this unless and until they knew all the questions they wanted to ask.

So far, their list of important unknowns was quite short:

- There appeared to be no external electricity supply cabling or local generating equipment
- There appeared to be no air intakes or outlets
- How big does the bunker need to be? Noting they mostly were sited in existing caves or similar ready-made deep spaces

Claud and Chess spoke frequently over their secure line, and they began to realise that providing long-term, independent life support in bunkers and in space travel presented the same problems, food, fuel and time. How have they solved these problems? They could solve the food and fuel issue if they had enough energy, and clearly booster rocket stages and additional fuel tanks would not do the job. There was, at this time, no solution to the time issue and current thinking is around freezing people for a long term while radiation on Earth dies down, or the spacecraft reaches its destination planet.

As their talks progressed, they realised that there must have been double and triple subterfuges at STP Industries in that they must have solved the nuclear fusion problem and were applying it to the space rockets and bunkers. It became patently clear that Professor Wu Lee had been hoodwinked in that after sending his fusion plans to STP Industries development and production facility in Palo Alto, far from mothballing the project, they had completed it without his help. The plans must have been sufficiently detailed to enable others to complete the work without Wu Lee's further help which was vital as they did not trust him, both from his reputation and his attempts to talk to others in the company. Chess went back to the photos Sam's boys had taken in Ulara,

"Look at this," he told the others, "We missed what is staring us in the faces by reason of omission; there are no booster rocket sections or auxiliary fuel tanks, the rockets must be powered by nuclear fusion."

Chess, Claud and Jim got together in their Boulder City secure warehouse and after a short discussion agreed that Agenda 2 and Agenda 3 were not just the controller hedging his bets, it always was just one big scheme but with complete segregation of sections to allow for part to be discovered without jeopardising the whole plan. One had to agree, the controller was a genius.

The Countdown Begins

There were 20 bunkers in all, and Claud had found 19. Claud began,

"We have found 19 bunkers that fully circle the earth, so there need not be a 20th but no one would build 19 and not 20, there must be a 20th. I have no idea where it could be and my teams have wasted enough time looking for it. So, we will stop the search but keep our eyes and ears open just in case," and the others agreed. It turned out that they would find the 20th bunker in due course, and it will become of key importance to them. It was under the rock at Uluru, with a tunnel entrance 100 metres away hidden in the scrubland. Unless you knew it was there you would never find it, but the aboriginals did and until the steel main doors were fitted, they entered and left at will but caused no harm, they were just curious. What they did not know was that once the doors were installed, the

96

tunnel was extended in two directions, one right under the centre of rock and one towards the Ulara facility.

They were divided up bunker or space rocket, asleep or awake, which bunker or which rocket (by rocket number), paired or alone, and so it went on. There was a bias towards scientifically oriented pioneers joining the space group but other than that most got their choice. A few complained and attempts were made to accommodate their wishes, although in the end, a few did not get their choice. They were given the option of accepting where they were put or leaving the pioneer group. It was all reminiscent of the loading of Noah's Ark.

However, by now most knew that all was not as it seemed, and it was generally understood but not talked about that there was no rogue third force intent on destroying the world, it was all about the concept of the pioneers themselves, which was still exciting and a good reason to stay. Besides if you left and the destruction of the world was real regardless of who caused it, you would signing your own death warrant in which case, staying with the pioneers would be your only chance. So, whether or not the world was to end, staying with the pioneers was the obvious choice and no one opted to leave.

The move began, in groups they were spirited away from their home and allocated to their respective locations. The space rocket inhabitants stayed in the 20th bunker alongside a small group of mainly technicians who were to remain in that bunker as its long-term inhabitants. It was another 20 days before they moved. They were taken through a tunnel that took them to one of the big hangers in Ulara, but they were given no clue as to where they were except that they were by the rockets which were massive. This would be their home until blast-off, whenever that would be. It had to be soon, and they were all nervously excited.

At some point during their stay in the hangar, the pioneers were visited by a strange cloaked and masked figure all in black who gave them what can only be called pep talk. He was clearly in charge of everything around them, but he gave no indication of his name or anything about the overall aims of the venture. From then onward it was a question of waiting and practising for the launch.

Peter's group was sited in the Northwest of Finland below one of Finland's highest peaks at just over 1,000 metres. He did not know whether their cave was natural or man-made, but he assumed it was a combination of both. The tunnel from the entrance was about a half kilometre long descending along its entire length which he assumed must be man-made, while the cavern it opened out into was gigantic and looked natural. They were clearly near the centre of the mountain and several hundred feet below ground level. So, this was to be his home for anything from one year to 100 years, but being one of the staying awake group, he realised that in all likelihood, once the doors closed, he would never see daylight again. Strangely, in the front of his mind was his broken Volvo P1800. If only he had not crashed it again; if only he had had the time to complete the rebuild.

D-Day Minus 40 Days

Those thinking they were in charge and those really in charge were all pondering the same problem, what to do about the Ulara facility. They wanted it smashed, razed to the ground, all bombs removed, all radioactive material removed, but they could not for a number of reasons, each strong on its own but taken together, overwhelming.

- The facility had broken no Federal or State laws in Australia
- There were now over 1,000 people somewhere inside, they would have to be removed forcibly or voluntary before any attack took place
- It had proven strong defences and it was assumed by all that there were even stronger defences as yet unseen
- The facility was in Ulara which is near the sacred Aboriginal site of Uluru. Ulara is within the bounds of the sacred land that the Australian government has given back with a promise not to interfere. So, Aboriginal approval would have to be gained, which would never happen
- The agreement with the Aboriginal leaders was that STP Industries would leave the site and put it back to its natural state and remove all traces of technology, equipment and occupancy at the end of the agreed period. The end date was less than two months away.
- If there were nuclear weapons and bombs at the facility, then to attack could set off a very big bang also rendering the land for many miles around to be uninhabitable for up to 100 years.

So, they decided to wait and see – which seemed rather pointless if one of the only two options was death to all humankind.

Chess believed that the only way to take down the facility would be with the help of the Aboriginals, it was their land, and they were at home in it. They have proven that they could get in and out of the facility at will without being discovered. No one else has achieved even getting to the front door and many a tenacious press hack had tried.

Chess met Sam had asked the Aboriginal council for help in getting them inside but also warning them of the dangers of precipitative action. They needed a workable plan and it was Sam who spoke first, taking everyone by surprise by starting at the end and working backwards from there saying,

"After it happens, as and when it is safe to do so, the aboriginal council would be the first ones to enter so that we can reconsecrate the land as soon as possible. Before that we do nothing." The logic put forward by the council, perhaps naively, seemed to have only one downside as compared with the unworkability of all the other solutions they debated through the night. However, this downside was a pretty big downside in that it allowed the scientists to complete their work and fire off 17 rockets each containing bombs and 1,000 people. The trick was to ensure the bombs did not detonate. On the other hand, they were in danger of precipitating the cataclysm themselves unless they could disarm the bombs or remove the command-and-control capability.

While this would not be an ideal long-term solution, and with a sword hanging over the Earth, Chess commented positively,

"I am persuaded by the simplicity of this plan and, coupled with no other viable solution being at hand I will go along with it." Chess assumed that Jim and Claud would agree, and in any event, they still had some time to change their minds. Sam, clearly happy that the bombing of the Ulara had been stopped and his plan adopted, continued,

"I will send my men into the facility, to make contact with the 1,000 new world pioneers and gauge their reaction if the pioneer's journey was called off, and while there, we will also check on the rocket assembly progress." Chess called Claud and Jim Bray and related the events in Australia, and to Chess's relief, they agreed with taking the 'do nothing' approach even though it had the biggest risk, i.e., letting the rockets launch. The name of the game now was to find the command-and-control centre and destroy it, and from the timescale of the STP Industries lease agreement, they have less than two months to do it.

The Cocoon

Julie and Jacob had no idea when it would happen, and their only clue was the activities of the pioneers in the bunker. Julie had traded her pride and joy, her BMW Z8 for a canvas-topped small truck, old and diesel because she understood diesel engines from her work and she reasoned if any of the modern car electronics failed, she would not be able to fix them or acquire spare parts.

She told her friends that her BMW was getting old and needed a lot of money spent on it. The reason for the truck, she said was because she was building a getaway cabin out in the country as a bolt hole. She implied very strongly that it was to get away from her husband, which friends believed as they were aware of her situation *viz a viz* their marriage.

But the real reason was to hide Jacob on their trips to the pioneer bunker, and it was useful to keep prying eyes away when they purchased goods for their bunker which they gave the code name 'cocoon'. Some six months after starting their unlikely partnership, they saw the pioneers beginning to act differently. They came out of the bunker mainly in twos, man and woman, couples, and they were taking photographs of each other as well as many of the countryside surrounding the bunker. There were no more crates or other goods arriving, clearly, so they must be getting close to the big day.

Their cocoon was just about ready, and a certain respect and trust had built up between them, not quite friendship which they both thought a step too far. An incident had occurred a month ago which served to show how far they had come in breaking down the racial barriers between them. They had agreed on separate living quarters with a shared main area. Each private area had a stout entrance door with a strong door lock. The key to each lock was held by the person whose area it was. They soon realised the folly with this arrangement, if someone was taken ill inside their locked 'apartment', there would be no way for the other to get in and help. So, they both had keys to the other's private area. In the end, they did not bother to lock their doors at all unless one or the other wanted privacy. This level of trust could not have been contemplated six months ago.

Since it was 1.5 km to the surface and a similar distance down to the main workings where much of the equipment they needed was kept, Jacob proved to be invaluable in bringing equipment to the cocoon as they could only use the lift when it was not in shift use, which was not much of the time.

They needed to think about how long they would have to stay in the cocoon as this would affect their requirement for stores. Radiation was the big unknown, the level could dissipate very quickly if it was low level and the weather conditions were wet and windy, which would be likely after a nuclear explosion. Alternatively, if for example, the bomb was adulterated with cobalt, it would have a half-life of 50 years and it would be 100 years before it would be safe to go out without wearing a radiation suit. In the end, they decided to equip for one year.

To be safe they acquired, bought, stole or borrowed all critical equipment in triplicate. six radiation hazard suits (three small, three large); three diesel generators for electricity; fuel oil for a year; canned and dried food; three industrial freezers; three fridges; spares for the truck if it survived a nuclear blast (fuel pump, glow plugs, belts, tyres, etc.); three air compressors; 20 compressed air cylinders; heaters and a free-standing air conditioning system; a whole pharmacy of medical supplies; clothes and personal items, as well as of course, toilet rolls. In their view, they had to prepare for all eventualities.

Their main concern was for air and water, there was plenty of water in the mine being kept at bay by pumps running 24 X 7. They assumed these would stop when it happened and the water would rise up, but not by 1.5 km. The water was naturally filtered by the rock and was perfectly drinkable. The immediate problem was to access to it not knowing its level.

They tried as best they could to hedge their bets. They built some storage tanks large enough to last them a month, and they also modified the outflow from one of the lowest level pumps adding a diverter and new piping leading to the cocoon allowing them to tap off the water at will. They nearly got caught assembling the modification but managed it and redirected the outflow back to its proper place just in time. The diverter and new piping were not discovered, primarily because no one was looking for them. The one month's supply of stored water would give them time to repair and restart their modified pump or failing that, get at least one other pump going and move their diverter to that pump. There were plenty of spares in the mine store at the lowest level and they availed themselves with whatever they needed, treating it as relocation, not theft.

Indeed, on the question of theft, you could take anything you wanted with ease, even gold, but there was no way you would get even a grain of gold out of the mine. Checking at the entrance for anything coming in that could light a flame, say a box of matches, was thorough and checking on the way out was so thorough as to be embarrassingly intimate. For this reason, only whites were used as checkers, men for men and women for women and they were changed every 3 months. This played into the hands of Julie and Jacob, who were never challenged. The only problem they had was sneaking matches into the cocoon from outside. They achieved this when a checker caught a man bringing in a box of matches which he clearly forgot he had. Being black he was given a severe beating. Jacob saw his chance during the ensuing melee and picked up the offending item. Since he had already been checked, he entered the mine without further trouble.

They assumed that after the "big bang" the mine would be cut off from the surface and there would be survivors among the miners, just like the two of them, although they did not expect anyone else to have prepared their own cocoon. They were the only ones raiding the spares store. Those left living would treat it as a mine disaster and try to climb their way out, only to die soon after they climbed out. Many would not make it as radiation pervaded through the upper levels. They agreed to wait a week after the event before opening their door. They expected there to be no one left alive in the mine, just dead bodies. What else could they do?

They could not assume those still alive after the event would clear a path for them to climb out, so they had to make their own plans. They had to also take account of radiation and be prepared to come back to the cocoon quickly, all while wearing radiation suits. They would have to examine what was left and what blockages there were, but their current thinking was that they should try to assemble a construction site elevator along the outside of the main mine lift shaft, knowing that it would be knocked out by the explosion up top. If they could manage that, it would mean they could keep the cocoon as their base and travel up and down with ease, especially if bringing food and tools down from the surface.

Air was a big problem as it inevitably would come from the surface where it would be contaminated by radiation. It was Jacob who came up with a potential solution. He pointed out that the mine was vast and full of air. With just two people alive in the mine, they could live clear of radiation for years. All they had to do would be to set up the emergency air pumps in reverse so that rather than operate as designed and draw fresh air into the mine, they would pump air out; not too much but just enough to create positive air pressure in the mine, stopping bad surface air from coming in. Again, the problem was would the pumps continue to work? There were emergency pumps at every level, so they felt they could get at least one going.

Surface air would eventually filter down the mine and they had no way of knowing how long they had. All their plans were geared toward a one-year stay. Would that be enough? Could they last that long in the cocoon?

When they felt they had done enough to meet their needs for the immediate post big bang period, they began to talk about boredom. In fact, they had never been bored when in each other's company as they had so much to learn from each other given their totally different lives from birth. They realised they had been indoctrinated throughout their lives and step by step they were freeing their minds. Perhaps the biggest surprise was Jacob, he was highly intelligent and well-read. He had taken on the persona of the strong dumb one having learned at a young age of the perils of being black and putting your head above the parapet.

They each chose books, games, videos and jigsaw puzzles to keep them amused and jointly brought in some exercise machines to keep them fit during their year in isolation. They also chose schoolbooks and textbooks covering specific practical subjects, both to educate themselves during their lock-in period and also, if needed after they came out since there would be no one to ask for help when a problem occurred.

Thought turned to the aftermath, would there be anyone else alive, would there be vicious gangs as depicted in so many cataclysmic movies? Would they need money, what would they eat? They decided they could do no more and resigned themselves to whatever the future held. For money, they would use gold, but they could not get it now, it was too well protected, instead they would mine it directly out of the rock if and when they needed it. They had a whole gold mine to themselves.

Now all they had to do was wait and keep on observing the pioneers in the bunker.

D-Day Minus 30 Days

Just when they thought the tide of government and public opinion was building up to full acceptance of the situation by both government and public opinion, everything changed. Bombs were found in almost all the major cities of the world, not nuclear but nevertheless large. One had been found in Washington DC stacked in a corner of the Lincoln Memorial. In fact, it was too easily found, and too easily defused. Not only that, the first bomb led the way to all the others.

Chess and Jim Bray were highly sceptical and felt it was a deliberate distraction away from the real target as well as a way of undermining those doom-saying the end of the world is nigh. And it was working. Security agencies went into CYA mode and governments backed off into a wait-and-see position. Never mind the bunkers, the 10,000+ Pioneers, the rockets and all that was happening in Ulara. And they had not yet found the command-and-control centre. They were clearly losing the game, but it was not over yet.

All this made those not believing the predicted end game, clamour to have the Ulara facility stormed and wiped out, so putting an end to the whole thing, STP Industries, nuclear weapons, rockets and all. Chess knew only too well what would happen if this was attempted. But there was no point in trying to talk people out of their new-found complacency, so he went back to Ulara where things had moved on in his absence.

There were now two apparently half built rocket gantries in place. Did this mean they are not ready and would need at least another two weeks? But his hopes were dashed when his Aboriginal 'scouts' described what was going on in the hangars which told him there was only one piece to the rockets, no add-on booster section and no side-pod fuel tanks. The rockets were ready and so it seemed were the launch gantries, the other half of which was bolted onto the rocket. Chess could see now how it would work – a 'plug and play' rocket launch system adaptable to any size or shape rocket.

But a rocket without additional fuel tanks and boosters, how could the work? Re-fuel in space from a space tanker or space station – Chess would not rule that out but thought it unlikely. More efficient solar panels and a reliable, controllable ion drive system – yes to the improved solar panels but the ion drive was years away, or was it? Last of all was nuclear fusion. This was Professor Wu Lee's speciality, and he would tell anyone who would listen that he had solved the problem. Chess swore under his breath, he was sure that was it. Not only would it solve the rocket's problems it could also power the bunkers for as long as necessary.

Chess seemed to have arrived just in time, there was activity going on to get two rockets ready for launch. Lights went on at the launch pads, the hangar doors to the smallest hangar opened and two rockets were rolled out. His local team told Chess that these two were substantially smaller than the 15 others and it was patently obvious that there would be no room for passengers. Suddenly Chess was aghast, there were no windows, no doors, no docking hatch and no re-entry heat shield.

- these were not spaceships, they were missiles!

The missiles were loaded onto the gantries, the two halves fitting together perfectly. There were some cursory checks then everyone retreated into the open hangar, the floodlights were turned off. All was quiet again just as if nothing had happened except there were two shiny metal tubes reaching for the skies. By now Wu Lee had worked out what the other two small bombs were for, but he did not know where they would be targeted.

Chess called Claud and Jim Bray updated them and told them to get to Ulara as fast as they could. They needed a plan and a way to put it into practice and time was now running really thin – they had hours or at best days but certainly not weeks. As soon as the others arrived, they all asked each other the same questions:

- What were these two-maverick rocket/missiles?
- Where were they aimed at – space or places on Earth?
- What is the payload?
- When would they launch?
- What could they do about it?

And so, they went on with the launch becoming more imminent by the hour.

D-Day Minus 15 Days

The longer Chess stayed in Australia the more he liked it, but he had no time for tourism. Indeed, the pace had suddenly hotted up. A figure in a black hooded robe and wearing a facemask had arrived. The person responded to the name the controller although to Chess he looked just like C&L's Mr Big. Were they one and the same person?

Whoever it was, he was clearly in charge. He spent the next four hours touring the facility, occasionally giving orders for some change or other which was instantly acted upon. He also spent half an hour talking to the "pioneers" who all seemed very happy.

The next day the controller repeated his tour and this time found only one item to comment upon. The workman handling the item was immediately replaced and 'escorted' away. When he had finished his tour, the controller indicated his satisfaction with how the project was going especially at the Ulara site.

Why was he here? Did this mean things were going to happen imminently? If so, were Chess, Jim and Claud any closer to stopping the cataclysm? Chess was short on information and that had to be his next move. He would use the aboriginal team to get him into the facility at night so that he can talk to the pioneers and examine the two prepared rockets as well as the look at the other rockets in order to assess how close they were to launch capability.

That night after being brought to the pioneers, Chess had a not-very-satisfactory meeting with them. They all appeared to be very happy and looking forward to finding a new home. They saw no risk or downside and had no concern for the plight of the rest of the people on the planet Earth. Clearly, they had been brainwashed and Chess would get no support from them. He later realised that the Pioneers, rather than being brainwashed, had been told the truth; they were not going to die but everyone else was. Their attitude towards others who were not pioneers was quite understandable.

Getting to the rocket launchpads was more difficult than getting to the pioneers. There were searchlights scanning open land between the rockets and the buildings, and assuming you got to a rocket, there was precious little space in which to hide. His guides told him it was all about timing and that he should keep close to them. then they were off, tracing a zig-zag path, stopping and starting to avoid the searchlights until eventually, they arrived at the first rocket which was clearly an ICBM (inter-continental ballistic missile); an unmanned, go-anywhere, flying bomb. Not just any bomb, it had a nuclear warhead. This was not destined for space but was a surface-to-surface missile.

It could stir up a major war; such a bomb dropped on Russia would be assumed to have come from the US and *vice versa*. And there were two rockets, so hit both countries at once! Then he was pulled away by his companions and taken out of the facility. There was no time to visit the second rocket, which did not matter as Chess assumed it would be the same. Much more important, he was not able to cripple either the bomb or the rocket. They would have to return the next night to do this.

Chess called Jim Bray and brought him up to speed. Was this a diversionary tactic or the main game? They both agreed on the former. Time was running out; the rockets were ready, and they supposed the delay was to give the Controller time to get back to his command-and-control centre. They were running out of time, it had to be the next night and Jim promised to get information on the best ways to cripple the bombs and the rockets.

But they were too late.

D-Day Minus 13 Days

Sergei Bucholova was a worried man. He assumed that it was the controller taking his revenge at last, but to kill Serrano in that terrible manner told him all he wanted to know about his impending death. Run! Was the only solution. He had money stashed everywhere but could not make up his mind. Then he puffed out his chest and proclaimed,

"I am Russian, I will go home where I can be comfortable." Yes, he would go to Russia, he had never heard Russia mentioned at STP Industries or at C&L Corp so maybe they were not interested in Russia implying very strongly that the controller was not interested.

And he was right, the controller was otherwise occupied, the two Russian bunkers were in place and occupied, and he had quite forgotten about Bucholova. So Sergei Bucholova fled to Moscow where he could get lost in the crowd. He was happy again.

War Averted

Wu Lee knew what was going on, his time, his work, his liberty and health had all been affected by this job and being made to create meaningless demonstration bombs to set the world at each other's throats, all to hide was really going on, did nothing for his self-esteem. He was a broken man both physically and emotionally, and much to his self-loathing, he began to take it out on his woman. He was even more incensed that far from rejecting his fusion designs they had been taken up and built by someone else, not him, and used to power the spaceships and the bunkers. And Serrano was still around to torture him again. He could build a bomb to kill a million people but could not stop this monster.

During that period leading up to the deployment of the 15 satellites and their payload, the only time he smiled was when he heard that Serrano had been killed and the manner in which it was done.

He stopped abusing his woman and actually started being nice to her although there was no undoing what had been done to her.

He would get his revenge for all those actions against him especially when his work was the key to the whole enterprise. He knew he was not being given a place in a bunker and would die but strangely he did not mind. Wu Lee had never met the controller but knew he was a perfectionist who like him, wanted exactly the outcome he predicted. He decided to mess up the 'experiment' ever so slightly by reducing the power of the bombs by just 3%. He had done the calculations and knew what would happen, but the change would be assumed to be an error of some kind and not put down to him, besides he would be dead, and, in the meantime, there was no Serrano to interfere.

At approximately 2 a.m. local time a nuclear device exploded over Washington DC. The bomb was delivered by an ICBM coming from an unexpected direction, that is, not Russia or China. Consequently, there was little warning and only enough time to get the President and his wife into the underground bunker and command centre. Elsewhere, the devastation was horrendous.

With a knee-jerk reaction, that part of the Government and the military high command who had made it into the White House and Pentagon bunkers, immediately set in train retaliatory action against Russia. The ICBMs were already launched when the hotline to Russia rang, and an excited Russian president screamed down the phone,

"Iit's not us, it's not us!" screamed the president, "It was not us, someone is trying to start world war 3, the missile did not come from Russia, look at its path. Do not detonate your bombs over our country, we would have no option but to retaliate."

The US president was ex-military and ex-CIA. He had a good handle on world politics and believed what he was told and as a result, ordered the first wave of retaliation to harmlessly self-destruct, after all, he had plenty more. This sparked consternation in the bunkers with the doves and the hawks at each other's throats until the wall display showed another missile this time on track for Moscow. The US president called the Russian president,

"Get out of there, quickly., there is another one coming, not here but on its way to Moscow. It did not come from us."

"I have seen it," said the Russian President in a sombre tone. "I believe you." Then Moscow was hit.

Sergei Bucholova had lasted less than 24 hours in Moscow, killed by his boss's bomb. One could see a parallel with the American couple who wanted to escape WW2 by going to the most unlikely place possible, very small and out of the way. They chose Okinawa!

Naturally, China joined in; they insisted it was not them but warned it would take the strongest action without warning if it was attacked. Over the next 24 hours, the 3 powers came to the conclusion that this was the work of a third party, and each checked on those countries friendly to them that had nuclear capabilities. Iran, Israel, India, UK, France, Pakistan and a few other surprising possibilities. All were innocent of the crime.

The US president remembered what General Jim Bray had told him that the bombs planted around the world which had all been found and disarmed, were a distraction and nothing more. Although not inclined to believe him, he had taken action against STP Industries and thought that was the end of it. Now, he was inclined to believe Jim was right after all.

The major powers group, formed when the last multi-bomb scare occurred and which set the powers at each other's throats, met with Jim Bray who came with Chess Chessington and Claud Liphook. The three set out their reasons for thinking this was another diversionary tactic, albeit greatly ratcheted up, implying that the real events were close to being set in motion, that is, the destruction of the earth. The group started down the path of recrimination but soon realised there was no time for that. They had only one question, what can they do to stop the horror from occurring? The nukes were sent as a warning to show they meant business and have the capability to make it happen – soon.

The thing that Chess and his colleagues did not understand was that all along they had been told or left to easily find out what was happening rather than do the whole thing in secret which would have been less risky for them. Was this God telling Noah what was to happen? Or just a challenge of wits? Or could it be that they are being set up in some way perhaps even as an unwitting essential part of the plot – right from the start? Chess considered this and the hair on the back of his neck stood up.

They turned to the problem at hand; they knew about Ulara and the bunkers as well as the existence but not the location of the control centre. Their prime aims were two-fold.

- Destroy the rockets and their payload without exploding the bombs
- Find the control centre and stop any signals going to the rockets and bombs.

Specialist teams had been examining the bunkers for some time now and had come to two main conclusions.

- They were all in deep cave or mines that would be impossible to attack without killing everyone inside and it would probably take explosives of nuclear power to do it. of course, this is why they were put where they were, stop the attack and live through a nuclear war.
- From the residents' point of view, they are so deeply embedded in the rock that communications with the outside world would be almost impossible. From Chess and the other's point of view, it meant that the command and control centre could not be in one of the bunkers, which was good news, although it meant they were no nearer finding it.

Their next consideration was the Ulara facility which led to major disagreements among the major powers group ranging from.

"Nuc it to the ground." Said some.

"Negotiate a solution," said others, but with whom?

Chess could see the logic in both, but nevertheless, he reminded them of their previous consideration on the subject which raised some key concerns about an all-out attack.

- The facility had broken no Federal or State laws in Australia
- There were now over 1,000 people somewhere inside, they would have to be removed forcibly or voluntary before any attack took place
- It had proven strong defences and it was assumed by all that there would be even stronger defences as yet unseen
- The facility was in Ulara which is near the sacred Aboriginal site of Uluru. Ulara is within the bounds of the sacred land and the Australian government had given this land back with a promise not to interfere. So, Aboriginal approval would have to be gained, which would never happen
- The Australian government was against it
- The agreement with the Aboriginal leaders was that STP Industries would leave the site and put it back to its natural state and removing all traces of technology, equipment and occupancy at the end of the agreed period. The end date was less than one month away.

- If there were nuclear weapons and bombs at the facility, then to attack could set off a very big bang also rendering the land for many miles around to be uninhabitable for up to 100 years.

It was agreed that as a first action Chess would try to meet the controller and negotiate a solution. Chess got on the next flight back to California and immediately and easily set up a meeting with Mr Big of C&L Corp which surprised him as the man remained a recluse and had seen no one since his last meeting with Chess who felt that this increased the likelihood of Mr Big being the controller and him being set up. They were to meet that evening at the C&L Corp offices.

D-Day Minus 5 Days

The same hooded figure as last time met Chess, was he also the controller? Chess decided to work on the basis that he was the controller. Chess explained that the world powers had accepted that the bombing of Washington and Moscow was set up to start World War 3 and that this had not worked. In fact, they were now working together to defeat the threat to blow up the world.

He went on to explain their dilemma. They could destroy all the bunkers, flatten the Ulara facility and arrest everyone involved and still alive after their take-out attack. However, that would mean killing tens of thousands of innocent pioneers which they did not want to do, so what would it take to stop this?

The man spoke,

"What makes you think I am the controller? Is it just because we both value our privacy and both wear the same uniform?" This did not deter Chess who knew that even if he was not the controller, he was very close to him. Chess replied with a simple request,

"Stop your countdown to oblivion, meet with the international task force we have set up and negotiate terms."

While this discussion was going on, Chess had a sudden flash of genius. SAGE had been called in to improve security at C&L; was this a ruse to stop detailed examination of all the service provisions at C&L including comms, payment systems, people and equipment tracking, and data security. The result was that they only looked for what was associated with the job at hand and since the command-and-control system could look like no more than a simple PC monitor, it had not been sought or identified. Chess would put the Weasel and Tam onto it immediately he got out of this meeting.

Mr Big declined to admit or otherwise that he was the controller, but he did come up with an excellent major point which he knew would cause yet more argument among the major powers group, Chess and his colleagues, which Mr Big referred to as an international task force. He said,

"If the world ends then billions will die, so why worry about killing a few thousand of these so-called pioneers? Surely it is a no-brainer." With that and without a goodbye, Mr Big aka the controller left the room, the interview was over.

As soon as he was out of the building, Chess called his team and told them he was sure the command-and-control centre was in the C&L building, so they are to go in find it and destroy it. SAGE still had its contract with C&L, and they had full access to the building at all times. It was now 11:30 p.m. but they understood the urgency and went to work.

At 2:00 a.m. Chess received a call from his team. They had found it in the comms room among the network of hardware racks. Rather than make it obvious they had destroyed it, leaving the way open for it to be repaired, they had encrypted the interface firmware, encrypted the control program, shorted and open circuited some key cables. The effect would be that anyone trying to use it would not be able to gain access through the encrypted software, but if they did, nothing they tried would get out of the command-and-control system and onto the network. In addition, they had installed their own 'babysitter' which would provide SAGE with notification of anyone trying to use the system.

Chess thanked them and told them it was a job well done. Would they now look elsewhere in the building as a cover for where they had been and what they were doing? At 7:00 a.m., Chess received another call from his team. As suggested, they had looked elsewhere in the building and had actually caught an employee red-handed syphoning off money from one of the company's few secure terminals able to access 'real money'. This would provide them with all the cover they needed. However, the main reason for the call was that they had seen a travel order, Mr Big was flying to Helsinki on the first flight that morning.

Although Finland is supposed to house the happiest nation in the world, as Chess's plane touched down, he did not feel that way. He was tired, jet-lagged, worried, scared and at a loss to know where he would go and what he would do when he got there, all rattling around in his brain at the same time. He went to the old STP Industries offices only to find it locked shut and with a realtor's sign forlornly hanging out of a first-floor window.

What next? The only link to the past was the realtor as Chess presumed the same company was used to lease the building to STP Industries. He did not bother to call he got straight into a cab and went to their offices. A pleasant middle-aged woman, thinking he was interested in the building was most helpful;

less so when he said he was not. Nevertheless, she gave the address of the one-man office rented by Mr Kowelski when they vacated their headquarters. No, she did not see Mr Kowelski, everything was done remotely. Chess quickly thanked her and left.

Another cab ride and another part of town, dropping him outside a serviced office block. A matrix of bellpushes stopped him from entering. He looked down the list of names adjacent to the bellpushes; no STP Industries, no Kowelski but there was one that took his breath away – Chessington! Were they having a joke at his expense? was he the fall guy? He readied the gun in his pocket and took off the safety, pressed the bellpush and waited. It took about 30 seconds and the door buzzed. He walked in.

The location board showed the third-floor East wing. Despite the lift being already at ground level, and his tired legs, he walked. His only concern was what if there really was a Mr Chessington in that office, how would he know and in a moment of hesitancy, he would be killed. But his fears were soon allayed. He walked straight in without knocking and sitting at the desk was the familiar black cloaked masked figure. Chess did not hesitate that split second, instead with a single flowing movement he took out his gun and fired three times; all hit their mark.

He ran over checked the man was dead, took off the mask and saw a rather handsome, white thirty-something man, not the disfigured face he was led to expect. Then he was out of there, stopping only to drop the gun into the nearby harbour, then back to the airport and the next flight home. Once on-board the Boeing 787 he paused to take stock but instead he fell asleep and dreamt in the Dreamliner. They were three-quarters home when he awoke, and this time he was able to take stock. He had killed a man, not his first, but who was he, the controller, Mr Big, both or neither – a stooge? But he was in Helsinki in the STP office, so he must be the controller.

If he was right about that and having closed the command-and-control centre, surely by now they would have stopped the countdown? He should be celebrating but going round in his head was the recurring niggle that he was being used and everything he did was playing into their hands.

D-Day Minus 3 Days

Given the fact that the capitals of the two major powers were hit, thousands were killed, and the cities were rendered uninhabitable for years to come, it came as no surprise that whipped up by the media, the general public were blaming everyone in government, the military and the security services in the two countries. Riots were breaking out all over the US and Russia with the breakdown of civilisation a strong possibility.

After 10 days, the US had retreated from the edge of total collapse, halted by the emergence of a new group of leaders, politicians and military leaders, nine in all, who emerged from their bunkers and began to exert control. This was in fact a takeover of the country by a right-wing group, but it seemed to be the only game in town and was welcomed by both the right-wing supporters and the left wing, there being no alternative for them. In Russia, things had progressed differently where they had plans for such an event. There was now tight military control, and it was back to a Stalinist type of state.

Elsewhere in the world, there was similar unrest, everyone was scared. Contingency plans were put in place, which seemed mainly to be agreeing who would go into the nuclear bunkers when the next bomb hit. No country was immune to the fear. In unstable regions such as the Mid-East, the Balkans and Korea, the unrest broke into open warfare, peace talks were no longer of interest. There was also a mass exodus to Australia and New Zealand, as far away from the unrest as possible. But such was the clamour to get in that the two countries were forced to close their borders, and those that did get in were shipped to the empty centre of Australia; not far from Uluru.

The controller had clearly achieved his aim as amid all the insurrection, no one was chasing the real problem – until now. With the new, police state, governments of the US and Russia now firmly in control, the two historical enemies and most of the other members of the major powers group replaced their members with hardliners who came together to consider what was really happening and how much time was left. If the aim had been to create WW3 by setting the two biggest nuclear powers against each other, it had failed. But what was the point; why did they do it? They came round to the plot to destroy the world, but was it a reality? Was this a precursor, a try-out or just a distraction to put them off the scent? To their credit, they concluded that this could be the only possible reason for the bombing of their capitals, and they should talk about it seriously.

The new group members had not been involved with Chess and his colleagues working with the major powers group task force and called for an urgent meeting with them and the new task force. They all met in London, regarded as safe from insurrection and no less safe than anywhere else from a nuclear bomb. Jim Bray and Claud Liphook both hated those they were now working with, but the safety of the world was more important.

Chess briefed them on the death of the controller and finding the command-and-control centre to which everyone sighed a sigh of relief. But Chess cautioned care. He had no proof as to who he had killed and no knowledge that the command-and-control centre he found was not a dummy, a red herring, or one of several centres. Nevertheless, he did feel better now, they were getting close to the truth.

Ulara remained the key concern. The international task force now represented two major totalitarian states and they showed it. They wanted to attack it immediately, regardless of having no intelligence about the site defences, not caring how many of the innocent pioneers they killed and not even caring if a nuke exploded, this was the middle of Australia – who cares. Chess added to the list, the Aboriginals and the Australian government. In the end, they agreed to go there and "size the place up" as the American team member said. They would go the next morning.

Cocooned

The diversionary nuclear explosions were thousands of miles away from South Africa and had little direct effect on them, but Julie and Jacob knew the end of the world as they knew it was imminent and they had better start their move into the cocoon for real. It was scary but at the same time exciting. One thing they could not have anticipated was looking their friends and colleagues in the eye, knowing they would soon be dead while Julie or Jacob would be alive, the one who depended on the colour of the inquirer. They had agreed right at the beginning that come what may, this would be a two-person retreat regardless of friends and family.

They were ready but were surprised to find the pioneer bunker was still open. After the nukes, they had expected things to happen quickly, especially the pioneer bunker going into lockdown and sealing itself from the cataclysmic events to come. The world was going on almost as normal while they, like others, had assumed that the bombings would cause retaliation, triggering a world war.

Had whoever started this made a grave miscalculation? Was their work building the cocoon all for nothing? Three days later, with the launch of the 15 rockets and positioning of 15 satellites in a low earth orbit, they knew the answer. The pioneer bunker was all quiet and the giant steel doors were locked.

The mine stayed in operation, greed winning over safety. However, many had quit to be near their families, some moving into their own prepared bunkers, some driving far out into the middle of nowhere, thinking that would help on the assumption that the cities and key industries would be targeted. Few thought this would be much bigger and that there would be no escape. The chaos and confusion helped Julie and Jacob as their absence was put down to another two people running scared. At the same time, they could be seen moving around the mine with few questioning them. Some had realised that the mine would be a perfect place to hide from any nuclear blast and started building their own cocoon, but it would be too little too late.

Julie and Jacob entered their cocoon and closed the door. They had said goodbye to the world they knew, and their big adventure started. They did not know when it would happen, but it would be soon. They had hidden a Geiger counter outside the door with a thin cable running through a small channel under the door so that they could monitor the radiation levels and know when it was safe to come out. At least, that was the theory. They settled down in their new home half hoping the world would not end and half hoping it would happen.

D-Day Minus 2 Days

They knew that time was short, the bombing of Washington and Moscow having reinforced that belief, but they did not know precisely when it would happen. The perpetrators would not want too long to elapse before their next attack, whatever that would be, so Chess and the team assumed they had days at the most not weeks. In reality, they had two days!

The team began to organise their plan, three plans – one by Chess, Jim and Claud, one by the Russians and one by the Americans. In the end, however, they all converged into one plan.

Stage 1 – bombing using conventional bombs

Stage 2 – ground troops to go in and deal with any defences remaining, take prisoners of all people there (the Russians had orders to kill them, but they kept silent on this)

Stage 3 – disarm any nuclear devices

Stage 4 – bomb the whole site into oblivion This plan had some flaws in it:

- It would take nearly a day to get a task force of troops there and ready to go
- The Aboriginals represented by Jonny and Sam were set against bombing their sacred ground
- The Australian Government had sent a task force to monitor what was happening, to ensure the land for many miles around was not contaminated with radioactivity, and to protect the Aboriginal community and their holy places

Chess hated it, they were his friends and had helped him, but needs must, and he found himself lying to them and saying they would respect their wishes. There was no time for anything else, he knew the world was going to end but many of the others there did not believe it.

The plan was put into motion with the first air attack set for the next day 24 hours from now.

Pioneers

Like a well-oiled machine, the pioneers loaded into their designated places without fuss or delay although those designated for the spaceships and to stay awake were rather appalled at the limited space available. How could they live like this for years? Those in the bunkers designated to freeze were dutifully loaded into their metal coffins and the process started. Those in the spaceships designated to be frozen were put into their coffins and injected to put them to sleep but were not yet frozen.

Things were really starting to happen now; the spaceships were readied in their hangers. The bunker doors were closed and locked set to automatic and put on a timer to stop anyone from trying to get out during the lockdown time, which could be many years. However, the bunkers were massive, almost like an underground city and no one felt closed in when the doors were shut and locked.

Despite Peter's thoughts and assumptions, which were proved correct, the actual effect of the doors being closed and locked gave him a thrilling sense of occasion. The biggest event ever was about to happen, and he would live through it; he was one of the chosen ones. And as a doctor, he had a real sense of purpose and responsibility.

The pioneer's adventure was about to start.

D-Day Minus 22 Hours

The task force had arrived, and the planes were in the air. Four hours to the first air attack; then it happened. The hangar doors opened and 15 rockets with their payload attached as well as part of their launch platforms appeared on motorised platforms. Fully automatically they drove to their launchpads and started to move into a launch position.

Chess and his group reacted quickly. The bomber force was asked to continue their mission but to hold fire when they arrived at their target and await instructions. At the same time, they released the ground troops to go in and cripple the rockets trying not to destroy the payload in case they set off the nuclear bomb in each one and to spare the pioneers in each rocket. They started with long-range armaments, firing at the base and gantry of each rocket from outside the perimeter but the guidance system on each missile seemed to be jammed and the missiles flew away harmlessly. However, from silos hidden in the ground retaliatory fire started up using Chess's missile tracks as their guidance and soon the attacking group was forced to retreat. The space crafts continued their preparations totally automatically with no one in sight and no one to kill.

The next approach taken by Chess's men was a direct forward attack, but they were forced back again by a curtain of machine gun fire which appeared to be unmanned. Jonny and Sam told Chess that they had warned of this and only his Aboriginal men could get in and at that, only single file. They could not safely get a whole armed task force in.

Like a firework display controlled by music, 15 rockets fired up one after the other. Five minutes later, the first one took off, and then one by one separated by five minutes. The last one took off just as the bombers reached their target.

D-Day Minus 6 Hours

Then all was quiet, no people, no guns, no retaliation. Jonny and Sam set up a monitoring station, but no one thought the rockets would do anything other than Chess had been told. And true to form, that's what they did, each rocket delivering its first payload in a pre-planned low earth orbit 160 km above the Earth. Then the rockets carried on with their second payload, the pioneers, to who knows where. In fact, they went to the dark side of the moon, presumably to shield themselves from the explosions when they came.

Back on Earth, two things were happening, both Russia and the US had been developing satellite buster weapons but neither had them ready. So, they started a race to finish them, knowing that they were already too late. Each power was developing both ground-based laser weapons and space-launched missiles, with the efforts of both parties looking very similar and both failing in similar ways. Clearly, the spy networks were up to speed which was more than could be said of the scientists who still refused to cooperate, even now.

The second action was at Ulara where the troops were going in, very slowly in case of booby traps, and there was no hurry now. They found a few white-coated dead bodies – superfluous to needs now and no locked doors. The control room was up and running tracing all rockets and monitoring their payloads, but there was no kill or abort button and besides the tracking system nothing else would communicate with the outside world. It was now a totally offline system. Had killing the controller and disabling the command-and-control system worked? Had they won? After the technicians had given the equipment a thorough examination, it was decided to shut it down. They stopped the power generators and removed the comms circuit boards. It was eerily quiet and there was no way Ulara could send any signals anywhere.

D-Day Minus 4 Hours

The world's press was keeping the public up to date, with information, some accurate, some fanciful and some lies. In any event, the launch of the rockets confirmed that it was really happening. There was panic across the world. Governments went into their (not so) secret war bunkers, many of which were stormed by angry crowds; looting was rife, and many babies were made. The bunkers would give some protection, but how long could people stay in them? the same goes for people who rushed into deep mines, and even nuclear subs were limited to years not decades.

Chess and the task force considered their position; they were probably in the safest part of the world but that would not save them, and what if nothing happened? The riots and the bunkering of the elite and political had led to a complete breakdown of control, even given the new masters in Russia and the US. The world was not a nice place at the moment. Was this too part of the plan?

D-Day Minus 20 Minutes

After the army had finished their search and clean-up, they set about placing explosives to blow the place to bits, but they were stopped by Chess, Claud, Jonny and Sam who asked for time for the Aboriginals to go in and reconsecrate the land. Although they did not know what was to happen, when it was to happen and of course, if it was to happen, no one saw any reason not to allow them in and they were given permission to enter but touch none of the equipment, just in case.

They were in the middle of their incanting in the control room of the complex when a noise interrupted them, it was a phone ringing, and it did not stop. No one knew what to do, they had been told not to touch anything even though all the technical control consoles were disabled and dead. But the phone would not stop ringing, so with a nod from his leader, the person nearest the phone picked up the receiver. A voice said, "ET come home."

D-Day Minus 0 Minutes

The book says "with one bound he was out of the pit" (Hemingway). Not this time.

- Michael Kowelski was dead, having died without ever knowing the true purpose of STP Industries and the controller whom he had never met.
- Although they could not be sure, the controller was dead.
- The command-and-control centre had been destroyed.
- The Ulara control centre had been put out of action.

Had they saved the world from an unknown catastrophe?

At 7:22 a.m. local time in Ulara, the 15 satellites in low earth orbit 160km above the earth, fired their engines and began an unstoppable descent towards earth. After 30 minutes at a height of approximately 30km above ground, each satellite ejects part of its payload and continues its descent to earth, reaching the ground some 8 minutes later.

At 8:00 a.m, all 30 thermonuclear bombs explode simultaneously.

- The 15 payloads ejected at 30km above earth contained 1 megaton thermonuclear bombs configured to emit a massive high-altitude electromagnetic pulse (H-EMP)
- The second payload of 15 X 100 megaton thermonuclear bombs exploded just above the earth's surface

Wu Lee smiled, satisfied, then died.

It is D-Day!

The end

126

Book 4
Resurrection

What happens to a planet when the whole surface is destroyed, maybe even more damage than expected will be caused such as the earth's orbit being moved, and its rotational speed changing. We can only hazard a guess at the effects. Assuming it was just the surface that was affected, will the explosions affect the make-up of the air, rendering it impossible for humans and animals to live there regardless of the radiation level?

Interpretations of Gaia mythology indicate that everything is connected and a change in one aspect of our planet creates effects across all items forming the ecosystem that is planet earth. Consequently, we can consider a tipping point for damage to the earth, below which it will recover in time, but above which it will not recover and be destroyed. The assumption made by the controller was that his bombs would not take the planet over the tipping point and that it would recover, however long that took.

It is recognised that when the earth was created and had cooled somewhat, it was too unhospitable for humans and that different species roamed the land. As the earth cooled, the species of life adapted and changed resulting in what we see today. How would any species that was still alive adapt to the bombing that had taken place?

It is also recognised that the lower forms of life such as ants are much better at adapting to a changing environment than the higher forms such as humans. This has enabled them to have lived on earth much longer than humans, so will planet earth revert to one without the higher forms of life and be dominated by insects and the like?

We also have to consider the effects of climate change. Humankind was already being threatened by climate change before the blast, rising temperatures, rising sea level and wilder weather. What would be the effect of the blast and/or humans disappearing at a time when time the earth is undergoing significant climate change? Has the controller got it wrong and not sufficiently considered these cumulative effects such that his bombs would take the planet beyond its tipping point? On the other hand, man-made pollution and global warming will cease if there are no humans to create it and the world would recover. Was this the reason for the controller's action?

All was quiet and still in the world, but some flora and fauna continued to cling to life. Over the years, vegetation thrived without a man to stop it and slowly reclaimed the ground wiping out many of the signs of a past civilisation. Of course, radiation had taken its toll with most successful growth being mutations to the extent that little was recognisable for what it once was.

The animal kingdom appeared to follow a high-speed evolution path. The microbes and bacteria were unaffected and supported the next species up the food chain, the insects, spiders and the like who thrived and multiplied, apparently unaffected. In the sea, the plankton thrived as did the coral. Fish lived, the deeper they inhabited the oceans the better they fared with only the whales dying out completely. Some species of animal fared better than others and the offspring of most that survived the initial blast continued to live albeit strangely mutated such that some could not be recognised for what they once were.

Man survived in small pockets where the radiation had been screened for some reason, or in mines where the men could climb out without the aid of lifts. Because there was no communication, the pockets remained isolated for many years but strangely, all followed one of two similar paths. The hunter-gatherer groups forgot their past and lived off the land creating a new civilisation. The second group tried to remember their past, invaded what was left of the cities to reclaim books, found and used tools, hammers, saws, etc. They set up schools to teach their children.

Altogether, there were not more than one million human survivors.

In one respect, both groups acted similarly, initially, children born with defects were either not allowed to live or became outcasts like lepers in a leper colony. It did not take long before they realised that this was evolution in practice and unless they embraced all the people, their race would die out. So, humankind changed over the generations and thrived, and as it grew, so the closed enclaves spread out and began to meet each other. There were inevitable conflicts between the hunter-gatherers and the others, let's call them the townies.

D-Day Survivors

Julie and Jacob

Like everywhere without exception, Julie and Jacob did not have long to wait although they did not know what was about to happen up top and outside. Jacob was in mid-sentence,

"We have forgotten something, a means to know when it happens as well as a way to find out what it is like outside, shall I," and that's as far as he got; the ground shook and there was a tremendous roar,

"Dear god, it has really happened. We were right and we have a chance to stay alive, but what sort of world will we have to live in?" Julie was frightened. "Would it not have been better to die quickly than suffocate in agony from the radiation and all the pumps in the mine failing?"

Jacob remained calm and looked visibly shocked at Julie's outburst. Tears were running down her cheek and for the first time he touched her and hugged her. If he had done that yesterday, he would have been severely beaten and also receive a long prison sentence.

"Remember, this was your idea Julie, and together we have created an environment we can be proud of and live in. Look and listen, the world is dying, and we are still alive. I don't know about you, but I want to live and help create a new world where all people are equal regardless of race or colour. Now, wipe your face, we have work to do. By the way, what I was saying to you when the ground shook was that we had forgotten to install a means for us to determine what was happening up to and when the bombs go off. I was even going to offer to leave the cocoon to find a way to do this but all that doesn't matter now." He smiled as he finished.

Julie had never before even held the hand of a black man let alone hug him. Her feelings were all over the place, the world had been destroyed and yet, they were still alive and she had let a black man hug her be kind to her and for a moment, he was superior to her. She was ashamed, how could she fall to pieces just when she was proved right and they were still alive? She composed herself and tried to take back her leadership role but just said,

"Thank you, Jacob." It was the most Jacob had ever said to her in one outburst and the first time he had said anything personal. She was back to normal now and started,

"Right let's take stock, it has happened and we have no reason to believe it is isolated. I think that as predicted, the whole world has gone and we are among the few still alive, but for how long?" she trailed off as it had become almost unbearably hot in the cocoon.

"Right miss, I mean Julie, let's take stock then:

- We are still alive
- It is too hot, the room temperature is 120 degrees Fahrenheit or 50 degrees Centigrade
- If it gets any hotter, we won't live long
- The Geiger counter outside the door is showing a massive leakage of radiation into the mine
- The electrical equipment has gone haywire so the nuclear bomb must have also generated a massive EMP pulse

That will do for starters." Now Julie was back on song.

"Temperature, let's not start the a/c and use our generator oil on day one. Instead, let's set this temperature as the upper limit and use the a/c if it goes higher, assuming it still works. I hope that once all the surface fires are out and things settle down that it will drop to something we can live with. This is not the case for radiation and I suggest that even in this heat we put on our radiation suits. Finally, we need to check our air and water systems and pumps."

"You're the boss." Jacob smiled.

Some hours later, after they had completed their status checking tasks, still wearing their radiation suits they sat down feeling the effect of heat. Thankfully the temperature had not risen and in fact, might have gone down a touch.

"It is too damn hot in these suits, I wish we could take them off," Julie sighed and continued, "But the Geiger counter is going mad, even down here. Imagine what it is like on the surface. They must all be dead." Jacob nodded.

"We have working versions of all our equipment, you did good in insisting on three of everything. We lost quite a lot but not all three of any one item. We forgot to reverse the airflow to give a positive outflow. This might explain the rapid rise in radioactivity. Luckily, the air pumps support remote control and we included a controller in our inventory and I have reversed the airflow now, so hopefully, it will reduce somewhat. Water is not so critical as we have our own tank, but I can report the pumps are still running on normal flow. I have to go down to the pumps to divert the flow to here and I am not going out on day one."

They had three radiation suits each and quickly changed out of the ones they were wearing into new ones and washed out the ones they had been wearing. After a difficult meal due to the suits, Julie tried to keep up the good cheer remembering this is only day one of a very long stay.

"This reminds me of a story from the second world war that I have read about. In the second world war, a Japanese soldier on an invaded Pacific Island had become separated from his troop and was on his own in the jungle. He had been about to re-join them at their base camp when American soldiers attacked and overran the camp. The Americans set up their own camp and transported the Japanese soldiers to a nearby ship, leaving the lone Japanese soldier on his own. Should he surrender? No, he would not, and he retreated deep into the island jungle. He stayed there for 10 years, long after the war had ended and when eventually found, he took a lot of convincing that the war was over. Would the same thing happen to us? Might we go out after months in our cocoon only to find everyone going about the normal business?"

Jacob actually laughed at this story, another first for him, but then sombrely said,

"Radiation is going to be a big problem since it will persist for a long time, for example, the cobalt adulterated nuclear bomb has a half-life of 50 years, so we're talking about years down here, and even though the radiation is lower in our cocoon than the other side of our entrance door, and massively lower than up top, and we have radiations suits, we are going to be exposed and get sick. We must be prepared for this. and don't forget we will eventually have to go up top to scavenge for food."

On that note, they decided to go to sleep for the night but was it night or day? They had clocks but rarely referred to them, choosing alternatively to work when they woke and retire when they got tired. Although their sleep patterns were initially very different, after a while they seemed to synchronise and be awake together and sleep in their individual pods remaining in their radiation suits at the same time.

They stayed positive but neither in their heart of hearts held out much hope for their long-term survival. The radiation level in the cocoon had stabilised but it was still high enough to kill them. Nevertheless, they put on a brave face to each other and genuinely treated it as a challenge. The challenge was to stay alive!

After 2 weeks the temperature in the cocoon started falling and continued to fall for 3 more weeks almost touching 0^0C before rising to level off at about 16^0C. They deduced that firestorms must have blotted out the sun and that only the thermal capacity of the 1.5 km of rock above them had stopped a greater swing in temperature in the cocoon. It must have been extremely cold on the surface.

They managed 90 days before they took their radiation suits off for longer than the time it took to change out of one suit and put on another. They knew this day would come but were both scared about what would happen to them living in a high-radiation environment. It had stabilised and gone down a little, helped in part by their positive airflow system and partly by the storms raging on the surface about which they knew nothing. The mine water they had in their water tank had all but run out and they would have to leave the cocoon to divert the feed.

So, after 90 days, it was Julie who was first to mention the inevitable.

"We have to take off these damn suits and I for one will be delighted to do without it and sod the radiation." Jacob agreed.

"I have to go down to the water pumps to divert the flow in any event. I can do it with or without my suit and since I am going down the radiation should be lower. So I agree, let's ditch the suits but clean them and have them ready for when we go up top for the first time."

Opening the door from the cocoon to the mine shaft was treated as a big event by them and they stood to attention and saluted the event.

"I'm coming down to the water pumps with you on this first trip out and our first trip into higher radiation without suits. One of us may need help from the other," said Julie. Jacob nodded without saying a word. He felt odd, perhaps it was the radiation, perhaps it was the mine. He felt black again and subservient to Julie although she continued chatting on a one-to-one level basis, Jacob had gone quiet. The mine looked like a disaster area, which it was but the number of bodies shocked them often blocking their way. Jacob ceremoniously picked up each body and threw them down the lift shaft. After a while, there were too many and they just moved those in the way aside. All this with Jacob in sombre silence.

Once they got to the pumps, the job was quickly carried out and they returned to the cocoon, the climb back up being harder and slower than Julie remembered during her building phase when she came down to 'borrow' some equipment. It was the effect of the radiation, and she could see Jacob struggling like her. Once in and settled down for their daily main meal,

"Yes, I'm feeling it too Jacob but that is not the problem, is it?" said Julie to which Jacob responded,

"No Julie, it is just that once back in the main mine, I felt like the old Jacob working under a white boss, and I don't want to go back to that again." Tears came to Julie's eyes and she said tenderly,

"It's me, Jacob, I was your boss but now I am your friend and partner in staying alive. All that stuff of the past is gone, blown away by the bomb," and she added, "I'm feeling pretty rough and I am going to turn in."

"Me too, I don't like this radiation sickness and I hope we get over it or get used to living with it soon." But that was not to be.

The next morning, they both felt ill but Julie adopting her leadership role once again said,

"I know we both feel ill but there is nothing we can do about that and it will get worse. So, let's go up top."

"I agree Julie," responded Jacob who continued, "I think the radiation suits will get damaged on the climb out so I suggest we clear the way without them and put them on once we break through." They carried backpacks containing their radiation suits, water and some food but that alone weighed heavily on them. The mine was a mess and the higher they climbed the worse it got. They were forced to return to the cocoon and pick up a jackhammer they had stored in the cocoon and use up precious oil. Each time they returned, they had to rest up, but each trip they took was in itself a mammoth task, especially carrying the jackhammer. It took them two full days to clear a path to the surface, partly because their strength was being sapped by the radiation. There were plenty of bodies strewn around but nobody alive. What was clear, however, was that many had survived the initial blast only to die later from radiation poisoning, lack of food and physical injury. As they came upon dead bodies, they dropped them down the lift shaft to their final resting place some 3 km below ground level.

When they knew they had cleared a path to the surface, they went back to the cocoon to put back the jackhammer, rested up again, put on their radiation suits, and climbed the 1.5 km again before taking the final step out. The surface they found was the scene of utter devastation. Far worse than they had expected. Everything was flattened, unlike previous bomb-damaged land where remnants of buildings still stood like skeletal fingers pointing to the sky. Here, there was nothing. They returned to the cocoon in tears; what was the point of them staying alive; what had happened to their precious world?

"My god! It is unbelievable, what has happened to our beautiful world," exclaimed Julie, while Jacob, who had tears running down his cheek into his radiation suit, said,

"What kind of a fiend would do this to our world and at the same time kill billions? Are we the only ones still alive?" Both knew there had to be others but where were they and if found then what?

There were many bodies littered around, apparently trying to get into the mine in the hope this would save them. It would have been laughable if the situation had not been terrible, miners trying to climb out, others trying to get in. At first, they threw the bodies down the lift shaft of the mine, but this soon proved to be a monumental task and they were feeling pretty ill by then, so they just left other bodies where they were.

"Let's go home." Julie sighed and they both retreated to what was now their home.

They made three more visits to the surface each separated by 30 days, although their rest periods did little to improve their health. They took to wearing their radiation suits more of the time while in the cocoon and in climbing out. They raided the rubble that was a supermarket, a DIY store and a pharmacy, collecting food, tools and medications. So long as their health did not deteriorate too much more they could live like this for a long time but not long enough to outlive the radiation which had only depleted by a very marginal amount. On their second exit, they found what was left of a library and hunted through the rubble for medical books, especially for those dealing with radiation sickness and its treatment. This resulted in a further rummage through the pile of rubble that was the pharmacy.

"So, do you want to carry on or just wait to die," said Julie to Jacob when he was looking very dispirited.

"I am not going to give in to the monster who did this," retorted Jacob. "I will fight every inch of the way and I hope you are with me in this; after all the cocoon was your idea."

There was no longer any time to be morose for on their third visit to the surface, they came across people alive, six men and four women, all looking decidedly ill and ragged. One man, seeing Julie and Jacob in their radiation suits assumed they were pioneers from the bunker and became very angry. He made to come at them, but he did not have the strength, and just fell to his knees and cried.

"Let me help you," said Jacob as he moved forward to help the man up and being a white South African, he was startled to see a black face behind the visor of the radiation suit.

Julie explained, "My name is Julie and this is Jacob. We help each other and there is no differentiation between black and white. If you want our help you will have to accept that." The group nodded weakly and Julie continued,

"When the rumours about the destruction of the world started, we took it seriously and built a safe place 1.5 km below ground. We retreated into our cocoon as we call it and although some radiation is present, it is very much lower than out here. There will not be too much room but you are welcome to come down and join us." She had made the offer without asking Jacob first, but he nodded in approval.

The 10 all accepted with gratitude and it took three slow and strained hours for them to go the 1.5 km down the mine to the cocoon. Both Julie and Jacob knew that there was little chance of any of them being able to climb out. To some extent, the problem was solved when the three weakest died within two days of arriving at the cocoon. While there, the group all explained how they had survived, each one with a different story and each citing a miracle that they were untouched except for the radiation.

One man said weakly,

"We were dying on the spot, not knowing what to do and where to go and the effects of the radiation was making us wish that we had died in the blast. Then I found someone else alive and we decided that since we have been saved by the hand of god, we are meant to survive and we began to search for food and water. As we searched, we came across other survivors, and in the approximately six months since the blast, we have found about 20 others alive and who joined our group. But the attrition rate is high and as new people join, others die."

How these people managed to survive six months was a marvel to Julie and Jacob and everyone knew that of the seven survivors they had found, few if any would ever see the light of day again but they remained grateful to Julie and Jacob who, knowing the mine well were able to move them into new worked out caves and supply them with food and water.

It was in this environment that Julie and Jacob spent the years after the blast, gradually spending more time out of the mine as the radiation reduced. The weather was mostly wild, windy and stormy which may have accounted for the faster reduction in radiation than was expected. Instead of being down to the pre-explosion level in 100 years, it now looked like it would be 50 years. Julie thought that the lush growth in vegetation might also be a factor in reducing radiation. In the meantime, all those living in the world were suffering from the effects.

The mine became something like an inverted skyscraper, going down into the ground instead of up towards the sky. It was home to a growing community of survivors as it offered some protection from radiation and good protection from the weather. Julie had got all her stored equipment up and running, electric light, heating, cooling and cooking facilities, while Jacob was a natural leader for the doers, clearing rubble and bodies, building where necessary. Jacob, being black, had no trouble in leading a band of white men and a few black survivors. However, the black survivors had a lot of trouble treating everyone as their equal, but the necessity to band together to survive acted to overcome those indoctrinated views.

This insistence on equality, of most importance to Jacob, was personified when Julie and Jacob decided to live together as man and wife, although Jacob, being a religious man said they should formally marry if they ever had the opportunity. Nevertheless, Julie gave birth to a baby girl some nine months later. She was almost but not completely "normal", but no one bothered with that now. Everyone was not normal and they loved her.

One day, when Jacob and Julie were alone together, they started talking about the pioneers in the bunker they had found and used as their guide as to when the explosion would happen.

"About the bunker we found, should we tell the others or try to communicate with those in the bunkers?" said Jacob. Julie had been thinking along the same lines and replied,

"Jacob, what are the alternatives; we cannot break in due to the steel doors, and even if we did the high radiation levels still prevalent would probably kill them if any are still alive. Also, if we tell the others, in their anger they might block the entrance with rocks or use some of the mine's stored dynamite to blow the bunker to pieces, killing all those inside…" she paused for breath and went on,

"I think we should not mention the bunker unless someone else finds it. In any event, the next generation born after the explosion will have a more dispassionate view of the people in the bunker and who are clearly implicated in causing the explosion." Jacob nodded and finished the conversation by saying,

"Years, 100 or even 50 or perhaps just 10 living in a kind of rabbit hole is something I cannot imagine, it must be hell in there." The two nodded to each other and then went about their respective business, they would keep their secret.

Although Jacob and Julie had kept quiet about the bunker they had found, they often talked with other survivors who remembered the history of STP Industries, the rumours about it and an Australian facility, all of which was unfortunately proved true. Some remembered the pioneers, the group that Julie had tried and failed to join, being too old, and now she could see why. Nevertheless, it was what started her action to build the cocoon that saved her and Jacob and all that had happened to them in the intervening period. Some sought to look for signs of bunkers but not knowing exactly what they were looking for and with the landscape torn up, they came up blank. Besides, it was hard enough to stay alive and deal with essentials, there was little time to go exploring.

It was several years before one group of survivors came across what was clearly a bunker. It was a large cave entrance blocked by massive steel doors. There was no way that these people could open the doors and the thought of healthy people living a happy life just the other side of the door radiation-free, made them extremely angry. But after a while, they came to the conclusion that it was not the people inside who were to blame but the organisers of the whole exercise, blast, bunkers and all else that combined to almost destroy the Earth. Besides which things may not be going so well inside the bunkers, they may all be dead.

Like Jacob and Julie, most survivors knew little about the events leading up to the explosion, however, a few knew significantly more especially about the pioneers and the bunkers and in the frequent evening talks after a hard day's work it was a subject often raised. Just as Jacob and Julie had decided, it was agreed to leave any bunkers they found untouched at least until the radiation level was down to pre-explosion levels. Other groups had independently come to the same conclusion and when contact was made between groups, the survivors as a whole decided to wait and see. Given the radiation level and its decline, it was assumed that the bunkers would stay closed for about 50 years. Could anyone still be alive after tens of years in a confined space with no daylight? A few survivors tried and failed to break in but after a while efforts to get in were abandoned and the wait and see approach was taken by all.

Jacob and Julie lived for 20 years beyond the big bang and died within weeks of one another in their mid 50's which was considered a ripe old age for survivors. By the time they died, there were very few original survivors still alive, but there were many children and even some children's children. With old age being seen as less than 50, people grew up very quickly. The next generation was ready to rebuild the world.

What the survivors built initially was to no great architectural design, just private shelter since there had been very little privacy in the mine. People had become used to it and there was no longer any embarrassment about body parts and bodily functions, but privacy was still desired as something nice to have enabling the start of the type of individual thinking that leads to debate and from there to society.

If the aim of the controller was to wipe out humankind, conflicts and wars and then repopulate it with a new enlightened race, then he was wrong, very wrong.

Shaun

Shaun and his two colleagues were working in the tunnel one at each end with Shaun in the middle near the new station that was to be built when it happened. The lights went out, there was an almighty roar and rocks started raining down on him. The integrity of the tunnel survived, it had been built to withstand earthquakes, but the new station collapsed with its foundations falling into the tunnel, just missing Shaun. The ends of the tunnel had also caved in killing Shaun's two friends instantly.

But Shaun was in the dark in all senses. His LED headtorch failed as a result of the H-EMP pulse, but his old-fashioned, pocket torch worked. He could see what had happened and that there was little chance for his friends. He realised this was not an accidental cave-in but a massive explosion. Shaun, although easy to goad into a fight, was actually a cautious man and he sat down to gather his wits and take stock of the situation. In the meantime, shock waves and rock falls were continuing to happen and there was also a furnace-like blast which the tunnel mostly shielded him from, but the temperature rose to an almost unbearable level.

Just in case, Shaun called out loudly,

"Anybody there" and then forlornly, "Anybody?" But he knew he was on his own, at least in the area around the tunnel. Was it luck he was alive and everybody else dead, at least in the area around the tunnel?

He remembered his drinking colleagues talking about the end of the world precipitated by a nuclear war. If only he had listened. Nevertheless, for whatever reason, he knew this must a be nuclear explosion and that it was not the earth that had exploded since he was still alive. So, what was he to do, he quickly assessed the tunnel near him and concluded it was stable and would not collapse on his head, but the temperature was still rising and what about radiation?

He kept the onset of shock and panic at bay by telling himself the world is a very big place and they cannot all be dead leaving just him. No, not possible,

"Help, I'm here. Where are you?"

What was his alternative? He could not think of a better one and decided to stay where he was, at least for the moment and until things had settled down outside. What he could do was to access one of the still remaining fire emergency points which they had installed as their first step in working in the tunnel to install the ventilation system. It contained a full-body protective suit with a face mask and oxygen supply. It was not radiationproof but was better than nothing. Each point carried three suits and they had installed five points of which he thought he could access three, the others being too near the entrances and buried in the rubble. This meant he had nine suits each with oxygen for two hours, again better than nothing.

Also, he found that the emergency torches still worked (old tech, bulb and battery, no electronics). He also had his lunch box and water. All in all, he reckoned, heat permitting, he could last two maybe three days, although part of that time would be used in trying to get out. There was no escaping through the collapsed station, so he donned a fire suit and walked towards one tunnel entrance which took him longer than expected and left him feeling distinctly unwell, the radiation was already beginning to affect him. It looked like there was no getting out that way and he decided to walk to the other end to see if that looked better, but he changed his mind when he realised how weak he was.

Singing was his next defence. After going through many Irish songs including 'O Danny Boy' at least 20 times, he found himself consorting with the 'enemy', first America then England where he finished off in a fit of exhausted coughing with the final words from 'Land of hope and glory'.

"God who made thee mighty, make thee mightier yet." He laughed out loud, as sick as he was, he actually felt better. In the ensuing years, he did a lot of singing.

He retreated down the tunnel to get a little more protection from the radiation and took stock. If he waited too long, he would be too weak to break out. But the sooner he got out the more he would be exposed. In the end, it took him two full days to break out and by the time he was free, he was in a sorry state. He was also alone in being the only person alive among dead bodies littered everywhere he looked.

While breaking out of the tunnel, his mind had been occupied with the problem of where to go for protection and find food and water if everything had been destroyed and flattened. His best shot was a hospital X-ray department where he could find lead slabs and assemble them into sort of igloo, all predicated on enough of the hospital being left to find what was the X-ray department and access the slabs.

The nearest hospital was only a few blocks away opposite a pub in which he had spent many evenings drinking and playing pool and it took him nearly a day to get there. By now he was really ill, but he had a strong constitution and a dogged determination and somehow stayed alive. The hospital was rubble interspersed with dead bodies but fortunately, the areas that had been X-ray and MRI testing were easily recognisable and he soon found what he was looking for. He managed to find 20 lead slabs and 30 lead-lined aprons. Using broken wood from the rubble, he created something like a wigwam onto which he placed the lead slabs and aprons, then he covered it all with as thick a layer of rubble as his supporting struts could withstand. This would be his home for the foreseeable future. It turned out that he had chosen his location wisely as there were food and drink vending machines smashed but containing water, chocolate, and other goodies to keep him alive. He also found the cafeteria and took whatever had not been ruined, but there was precious little of that.

With all the time in the world to sit there waiting to die, his thoughts again turned to his precious world.

"Is it like this in the rest of the world? Why am I fighting to stay alive?" he talked to himself a lot for fear of losing his voice with nobody to talk to. He also knew the answer to his question, self-preservation is built into all humankind and he, like the fighter he was, still had plenty of fight in him. Perhaps he would find and kill whoever was responsible for all this. That thought helped him sleep at least, occasionally.

It was dark outside, not night as he first thought but thick smoke like the old-fashioned London smogs which he had read about, and the stifling heat had now turned into a freezing wind. Shaun rightly assumed this was the effect of the sun being obliterated and he hoped it would not last too long. In the meantime, he had some shelter from his wigwam. In fact, it lasted 3 weeks after which it warmed up to just over15^{0}C although it remained stormy and very unpleasant for so long that this weather could be considered as the 'new normal'.

Shaun had not thought of alcohol since the explosion but now he was resting, he remembered that he had frequented a pub across the road from the hospital before the explosion. Now it was an unrecognisable building site but there might be some bottles or cans left intact. It took him nearly a day but by the evening he had 'liberated' a stock of beer in cans and bottles, various spirits, boxes of crisps, peanuts and some chocolate. He would not starve or die of thirst. He got very drunk that night and stayed that way for two days. On the third day, or perhaps it was the fourth, he saw two people alive struggling along. Like Stanley hailing Dr Livingstone, they embraced as though they were old friends. He knew now that he was not alone and if there were two that had found him, there must be others.

Times were very hard at the beginning, few had the strength to do anything, while Shaun could just about scavenge for food and anything else of use they could find; he put it down to being in the tunnel and then his igloo or was it a wigwam? They formed a group varying from 10 to 20 as stragglers were found, and people died every day. But gradually they formed a core group of about 10 more able than the others and were able to settle down with the stronger helping the weaker.

After what must have been about a year, they started to have hope and began to make plans. Top priority was somewhere to live shielded from the weather, which was still continually stormy, although not as bad as just after the explosion. Second, on their list was food and water and finally making a start on recreating some sort of society in which they could develop. Radiation was not on their list because there was nothing they could do about it. They also discussed keeping humankind alive by having children, although the precursors had to be their top priorities.

Some months earlier, at Shaun's suggestion, they had made Shaun's tunnel their home after clearing the entrances. They made broken wood torches which gave way to battery torches when they could find them. Eventually they found some diesel generators which one of the group stripped of their broken electronics and got them going. Since the electric start no longer worked, they had to hand crank the diesel engines of the generators which was no easy task for the weakened survivors. They began to organise their scavenging into a planned daily task seeking fuel from smashed cars and trucks, and food and medicines from destroyed shops and warehouses. They were survivors.

They divided the tunnel into apartments which were allocated to one or more people as they wished, communal areas and storage areas. They felt that by then they should begin to preserve humankind and have children. Provided it was consensual, any of them could pair with any other and try to procreate. In the first years, there were many miscarriages, and of those born, 50% died within the first few weeks, but gradually the next generation was born and grew up.

Possibly due to Shaun's background and success in home finding, he became the *de facto* leader of the group, which could by then be called a commune. The one key decision this led to was that they would become townies rather than hunter-gatherers and strive to rebuild what had been lost. In doing so they ranged through the dead city of what was Albuquerque looking for intact or repairable equipment and possible manufacturing systems. They also came across two other communes with similar stories to tell. Gradually, individual people became groups, then communes, and then towns, they called theirs New Albuquerque.

When they made contact with groups of hunter-gatherers, after settling their differences, which in point of fact turned out to be more imagined than real, the rebirth of their local society became complete. Now they could move on to rebuild their towns, their cities and their countries. After 20 years, Shaun could look back and reflect with satisfaction on what he and his people had achieved.

Tony Silbeck

Tony Silbeck aka Rhino had killed Serrano, and as he expected, he was not one of the ones selected by the controller to be saved. He knew this, in fact he knew an awful lot about the project having 'listened-in' to all communications for many months. He decided he did not want to be grateful to the controller for his life and he would chance it on the outside. Like Julie and Jacob, he made plans on the assumption that shielding from radiation would be the prime objective with protecting against the blast the next concern. He based himself at CERN in Switzerland where the Large Hadron Collider was sited. It housed miles of underground tunnels and passages all well protected from blast, radiation and an EMP pulse which were some of the key reasons why it was built underground. He faked credentials there get a job with them and soon found himself at the head of a data analysis team looking for patterns in data gathered from LHC experiments. He had free reign to explore the facility and soon found his hideaway which he began to provision but as it transpired, being streetwise as a kid and analytical as an adult did not help him much.

He survived the blast and avoided the EMP pulse killing his equipment, but there was no electricity or communications,

"I must get out of here." he said to himself, "I assume from the lights going out that it has happened but don't know what. I should have provisioned my new home better than I have, at least so that I can find out what is going on." He knew what he had to do, leave his hideaway and go to the entrance.

He took with him a portable Geiger counter and tried to take a pickaxe from the nearest emergency point but his Serrano injuries precluded that. Worried about not being in control and venturing into the unknown, cautiously, he set off for the entrance. The radiation hit him just as he started to climb the stairway out, the lift not working as he had expected.

As well as the radiation, his Serrano injuries and the mechanical prosthetics resulting from them almost put paid to Rhino forever. But there were others who survived the blast in the same way as Rhino, who gathered him up and took him back underground. They were a logical lot and began to organise themselves into working parties to forage, look for other survivors and research radiation sickness and possible remedial drugs. Nevertheless, they all suffered much the same as all other survivors and had a similar death rate, but Rhino survived. When he was well enough, which was not very well, he told the group, now 25 strong what he knew about the plot and the bunkers, As well as the expectation that there would be no survivors. Someone had got their maths wrong.

Tony Silbeck only lived another 15 years, but in that time became a maths lecturer to those survivors who wanted to learn and a schoolteacher to the next generation children. He never regretted choosing to be survivor rather than a pioneer.

Pioneers

The Bunkers

The bunker pioneers had started their new lives well before the explosions, in fact, they never really knew exactly when it happened since they were so well protected in their bunkers. There was a short period of a few minutes when many of the electrical systems shut down but restarted. The life support was, however, unaffected and during that period there were some strong vibrations through the bunkers. It was assumed by those awake that this was it, it had happened, but surely the death of the world would be more noticeable than a slight vibration. The pioneers carried on their lives in the bunkers as 'normal'.

The pioneers settled down to their initial 1 year locked away in their bunkers and on the space station, although all now knew it would be much longer. Each pioneer location was to be set up as a democratic community, with a voted-in management committee. To start the ball rolling, a person in each location was designated as lead pioneer until the committee was voted in. Their instructions were simple, (i) once the main doors were locked to check out the basic systems, life support etc, (ii) to open the large operating 'bible' (manual of operating procedures and processes – MOPP) and follow it religiously, and (iii) vote in the first committee.

Peter was given that role in his bunker and after the door was closed, he went, as instructed, to the management room where there was a PA/communications hub and announced to the other pioneers,

"Hello, my name is Peter and I have been asked to manage the initial elections for the management of our new home. I suggest that we wait a day or two for you to settle in and explore the bunker which, from what I have seen so far, is more like a small town than a big cave." There was a murmur of approval then everyone just carried on with what they were doing.

Peter found his marked living space, unpacked, found a nearby café, had a light meal and then went back to the management room, which took him longer than he expected as everyone was introducing themself to everyone else. There was lots of hand shaking. The management room was just a committee room with a large board room table in it, some cupboards and a safe. The MOPP was in the safe, the combination of which he had been given but it was anyway open. He took out the MOPP and opened it but before he could start reading, there was a strong vibration like an earthquake and the power failed but restarted within seconds. This must have been it, the end of the world. They would save the planet and re-populate it.

Via the communications equipment in the room, Peter could see into the public places and saw some degree of panic among the pioneers. Locked doors, the unknown, he could understand it and as the first bunker manger, it was down to him to do something about it. It had been some 5 hours since the doors were locked and already there was a problem that if left unchecked could lead anarchy in the bunker.

Looking for inspiration, Peter started to read but as he read, horror swept across his face, he felt weak and dizzy and almost fainted. The truth that he knew but had pushed to the back of his mind was now down there in black and white, pre-planned all along. The text on paper at the start of the book read:

"Dear Pioneer, by now the world outside your bunkers will have been destroyed, you are the only ones left alive. 15 Cobalt enriched nuclear bombs were detonated from satellites in orbit in space. The shock wave and radiation will have killed everyone and everything outside the bunkers. In addition, an electro-magnetic pulse will have destroyed all electronic circuits outside the bunkers and much heavy electrical equipment resulting from very high induced electrical currents.

The half-life of the radiation from a Cobalt bomb is just over 50 years and our scientists estimate it will be 100 years before the earth is safely habitable again and the bunker doors can be opened. You, the pioneers will all be dead by then except for those asleep in their cryogenic chambers. Your children will be charged with awakening them when the doors open and then will look to them for guidance.

It will be your duty to have children in order that they may be the new pioneers to re-populate the world

Good luck."

Before this he had assumed it but now it hit home, and there was no going back, no alternative. They had been duped, one year had become 100 years and there was nothing they could do about it. They had been locked in for 5 hours with only another 99 years, 11 months, 30 days and 19 hours to go. To venture back outside was to commit suicide, and anyway they could not open the door to let out those wishing to do so, as that would allow radiation into the bunker killing them all. Peter thought, would he rather have been outside and killed alongside billions of others, or live what would be a miserable life, like a lifelong prison sentence, in the bunker. But he knew, humankind's natural instinct was to survive which told him he was better off where he was.

He looked at the rest of the MOPP, but it contained only operating instructions for the bunker. One thing was clear, the rumour that had been circulating among the pioneers before they entered the bunkers was correct. There was no rogue element trying to destroy all mankind with a 'good' organisation countering the threat by creating the pioneers and their new homes. In fact, it was one and the same group making the pioneers complicit in helping to destroy humankind.

So, his survival was entirely due to the people who had engineered and executed the disaster. Should he be thankful for them allowing him to live? Regardless, he, like most of the others he assumed, was determined to exact some sort of justice if and when he got the chance?

But what was he to do now? How would he avoid being taken as one of 'them' and lynched on the spot? Maybe he should not tell them, at least not yet; but that would put him in the position of power over the others and this was supposed to be an egalitarian community. He had to tell them now! With his mind made up, he went to the broadcast system in the committee room that he had spoken so brightly into only a couple of hours earlier, sat down at the desk and switched it on. He began to speak:

"This is Peter again; As I told you I am the designated initial leader charged with the duty of organising the election of the bunker management committee. I will do this shortly whereupon I will return to being just a pioneer and not seek and further role as a member of the management committee. The news is not good."

He paused, let them have it a little at a time. There was now a lot more murmuring. He had better get it over with.

"I have just read the document waiting for me in the committee room and it has made me wish that someone else had this role. The document sets down the role, remit and timescale for the pioneers and I will relay its contents to you, so stop whatever you are doing and pay close attention. Also, I would ask that you take no action until I am finished.

You will all have felt the vibration and power glitch of a while or so ago, that was the event to destroy our world and the reason we were put in the bunker. We were chosen to be pioneers. What is clear now is that the organisation bent on destroying the world is the same one that created the bunkers and pioneers to save it. We are all complicit in the murder of the world's population, billions of people.

We have all been duped, not just in this crime against humanity, but with our lives. The explosions you felt were from a series of Cobalt enriched nuclear bombs mounted in satellites surrounding the world. The shock wave will have destroyed most buildings and man-made artifacts killing billions directly and as a result of falling buildings. The radiation will then have killed everyone left alive. The half-life of radiation from a Cobalt bomb is about 50 years meaning that it will not be safe to leave this bunker for 100 years, not 1 year as we were told. I think you already knew that it would longer than 1 year, but 100 years is almost unimaginable. And they knew this when they recruited us!

So, what shall we do? There is clearly no hurry so let's take time to think, regardless of the obvious fact that there is no good answer, just a least worst one. I propose that we take a couple of days to think, then vote in the first committee and let them come up with what we should do. In the meantime, we should check our stocks of everything from food to sticking plaster and see how long we could last if needs must, as seems to be the case. We also have to think about those asleep, what will be the effect of adding 99 years to their slumber and will we have to take the decision as to whether to waken them early?

Thank you for your attention. I have put on all your screens the letter waiting for me telling me all this. until I saw that, I was just as much in the dark as you."

There was consternation among the pioneers, but to be fair almost all managed to keep their temper and Peter need not have worried about them 'killing the messenger.' After an hour or so, they began to form natural groups and get down to the job of seeing how long their stores would last etc. A similar scenario was acted out in the other bunkers.

The Bunkers: Each bunker was divided into sections, living, exercise, work and training, storage for use while in the bunker, cryogenic pods for those 'asleep', storage for when the doors opened once again and the life support system. The last of these was a marvel to behold, although very few got to see it. Centred around a nuclear fusion reactor were electricity generators, waste recyclers, air purifiers and air conditioning systems. Much of the technology was taken, redesigned and improved based on space station technology, but only workable as a result of the nuclear fusion reactor. That area could run a major city for 100 years without any need for additional resources. It had occurred to many over the years since the end of the world event that by harnessing this technology, global warming could be reversed and our climate put back into good order, so why did they destroy life on earth?

The living section was like a small town, apartments, shops (no money needed) which were mainly swap shops for clothes, music and videos, restaurants (very small bistros), a large canteen, a school, a hospital, communal areas and a lecture theatre/conference hall. At first this seemed amazing, better than the awake pioneers could hope for, but after a while it became monotonous as well as potentially over-crowded as the children began to come along; procreation being encouraged.

In order to tackle two problems at once, overcrowding and boredom, most of the bunker communities decided to expand their bunkers. Selecting locations furthest from the built-up areas, and pointing deeper into the cave or mine, they used hand tools to excavate. There was no rush, and they did not want to cause a cave in. The average excavation period was about 5 years followed by 2 years fitting out, mainly as homes but they also built a bowling alley in one and a full-sized football pitch in another.

This activity saved many of the pioneers from losing their sanity. Once they had completed their build and sat back to benefit from the fruits of their labour, about 10 years after their start, most of the bunkers elected to do another build if there was space. They did not want to dig themselves out of the bunker. And so, another 10 years passed by.

There was no police force as such and no army, and indeed, there was little need as there was no money needed and little to gain with nowhere to go to. The only problems were sexual, jealousy, and over-zealous activities with unwilling partners. However, the encouragement of mutual respect and an open attitude towards changing partners more or less put a stop to that, the mantra became 'wait your turn'. Death was also a non-event, even though, it was rare enough in the early years to be remarkable. Bodies were recycled and that was it, everybody knew that!

There was some degree of organisation, pre-ordained in large operating 'bible' (manual of operating procedures and processes – MOPP). A 10-person committee acted as the government and the judiciary. 5 were permanent until they reached the age of 70 when they could choose their successor, and 5 were voted in every 2 years. Since the MOPP was written before anyone had any experience in long term bunker living, the MOPP specifically left it open to the committee to change it as they saw fit. In practice few changes were made and even then, they were mainly addressing operating procedures where practice had highlighted better way of doing things. It was found when the bunkers were opened that they had all mainly followed the MOPP had ended up remarkably similar.

Population was a concern in both the bunkers and the space station. The controller and his team planning the end of the world had assumed people would need to stay in the bunkers and on the space station for 100 years, but as the 50-year point approached, the population had already exceeded that expected after 100 years. There was nothing in the MOPP about extending the bunkers and yet it was this that saved them. Was this the first sign that those who had orchestrated the end of the world had actually got something wrong? Although a small point, it actually caused serious concern among the pioneers. What other errors had been made? Would they be able to deal with them?

The Space Station

Pioneers on the spaceships and fully awake, having bemoaned the lack of living space on board their new homes, suddenly were yelping with delighted amazement. As the craft moved in behind the moon, thought to be in order to hide it from earth as well as protect it from dual terrors of the H-EMP pulse and the nuclear explosion, there appeared a massive space station which was to be their new home for the foreseeable future.

Who built it, when was it built, how long did it take, why had no-one noticed the build and the movement of equipment and people to build it? Was it built by aliens from another planet? So many questions and no answers were forthcoming or ever would be. 15 rockets docked and the pioneers disembarked. Everything had been planned to the smallest detail, rooms were allocated to the awake, the freezing process was completed for those who had chosen sleep, jobs and roles were allocated.

All they knew about the death of the Earth was a bright flash from behind the moon and a slight vibration from the shock wave. Electrical equipment carried on working and the pioneers got down to their new lives in their new homes.

Besides being somewhere for the space pioneers to reside in safety while their planet burned, the space station had been designated as a centre for scientific research, the absence of gravity and air making it an ideal location for research. Consequently, in selecting the pioneers to carry on board, those with a science background were preferred. The initial research topics had already been selected, however, the scientists would be given free rein to move in any direction they wanted.

Although large, the space station could still be claustrophobic for its inhabitants even though it housed a cinema, a gym and study centre well equipped with educational books and videos. Also, the coming together of the sexes was encouraged both to preserve/expand the complement of humans ready to return when the time comes, and to provide R&R to the pioneers.

The pioneers aboard the space station knew full well that this was not going to be a short trip, everything was set up for a long stay. Even though the space was somewhat constrained and claustrophobic, the pioneers living in close proximity to one another, they seemed to take the extended time period in their stride, whatever that would be. Their main preoccupation was with getting on with their research which made them less worried, they had been selected based upon their desire to explore space and being research scientists which was what they were doing.

They were in the best place to carry out research and soon got down to work. They had nevertheless been chosen such that there were twice as many women as men. The need for procreation had not been forgotten even for this group.

The Space Station: As far as the space-living pioneers were concerned, there were no others, no survivors. They were pioneers, the ones who would save the Earth. The Controller had planned the space station as a research laboratory and the space pioneers had been selected on that basis. But it turned out that some candidates deliberately indicated an interest in research just to be selected for the space group. As a result, only about 80% of its inhabitants supported becoming a researcher and this group were pleased to find they would be left alone to do the research they wanted with no-one looking over their shoulders and telling them what to do, although to kick start the work, some specific guidelines were provided.

The remaining 20% of the space pioneers had no interest in scientific research and would have been better off in a bunker on Earth but it was too late to exchange them for other pioneers interested in scientific research. Instead, the non-scientists were put onto space station monitoring and maintenance duties and after a while everyone settled down as happy as they could be given the circumstances. The scientists began extending their personal interests and learning new topics in new areas for them, which was excellent for their knowledge base but slowed up research somewhat. However, there would be plenty of time to complete projects at whatever speed work was carried out.

The space station pioneers had been given the same news that Peter had read out in his bunker, but their reaction was quite different. They realised they would all be dead before the they could leave the space station, get back to Earth and put their research into practice. So, they all knew they must procreate as soon as possible, have children, educate them and have them take over the research. Like the scientists they were, they drew up plans for 'together time', and ensured they swapped partners with each child born in order to best spread through the limited gene pool they had, noting the possible problems with close relatives partnering in the second and third generations.

Life on board the space station was similar to that in the bunkers but rather more controlled as a result of being in a relatively confined environment with no escape if something went wrong. The space station was run as a research facility with a concentration on astronomy, cosmology, and a search for life elsewhere. These, mainly practical activities were supported by a team of theorists and mathematicians working out of a facility in the space station set alongside the research facility, and which became known as the Very Open University after the UK Open University. Over the course of the time spent in the space station, that is, 50 years, great work was done by the pioneer scientists and their successors.

Daily life on the space station involved the non-scientists maintaining the space station, cleaning, repairing, and improving facilities where possible. Additional learning and personal development was encouraged for all. Classes were available by choice in many subjects, chosen before departure based upon the skills of the pioneers joining the space station; being idle was discouraged and work or further education was found for all those with nothing to do.

Children were placed in a creche from their first birthday until they reached 13 when they were classed as young adults. On the space station, they were allotted a topic and a research tutor as well as continuing their general education. Space teenagers had little time for anything other than scientific research although most joined into the 'together time' activities. All in all, the system worked pretty well.

Those on the space station had a specific concern,

"How would they get their people back to earth when the time came?" they debated among themselves. Of course, it would not be the pioneers returning to earth, it would be their descendants. What would they make of the world they find compared to what they had been taught? Desolation instead of great cities, animals, and fields full of corn.

Multiple journeys were the obvious answer to getting the space pioneers home but there were no launch sites with associated launch towers left on Earth, the explosions had taken care of that, so the rockets could not take off again to make a second trip. In the end it was decided that:

Some pioneers, if still alive, and some descendants, would stay on the space station, not wishing to have to work in a desolate land with no comforts or supporting infrastructure implying, in their eyes, that they would be almost back to the stone age.

- The space craft would be overloaded as much as was safe, which was roughly double the original payload, after taking into consideration the absence of the bombs carried aboard.
- Leave those frozen to remain frozen until the spacecraft were able to return to the space station.
- Wait for new space launch facilities to be built, then the rockets could return, the frozen un-frozen and all who wished to could return to earth.

0 NB

BC and AD were replaced by NB for New Beginning. Population of Pioneers 20,000 Population of Survivors one million.

The H-EMP pulse had done its deadly work silently and quickly. Planes fell out of the sky, lifts stopped between floors, miners were trapped with no way out and no pumped air to breathe, ships drifted like the Marie Celeste, traffic lights failed, cars and trucks stalled, power steering and brakes failed, crashes were inevitable. Hospital equipment intended to save people was now killing them slowly, all lights went out across the globe, both in the zones in daylight and those at the night where it was totally black except for the odd lighted cigarette and the many fires caused by exploding electronics as a result of very high currents being instantly induced in all wiring.

The effect of exploding just one nuclear bomb in space will vary according to its height above the earth and its size. The bomb used here was enough to knock down un-reinforced buildings, badly burn anyone out in the open and start some fires, but many will live. However, with 15 bombs at the same time, the effect would be catastrophic, but still, some will live at least until they succumb to the radiation.

Those in nuclear bomb shelters will have fared a little better. If the H-EMP did not result in their death, and the nuclear shock wave and fireball were overcome due to the design of the bomb-proof bunker, the radiation was sure to get them. Even in a radiation-proof shelter, leave the door ajar and the radiation will get you, shut the door and you will suffocate since all the air pumps will have been knocked out by the H-EMP and it will be pitch dark.

And since the bombs had been adulterated with Cobalt, the radiation would stay for 100 years, so what was the point of living? But some still survived.

With military precision, exactly 100 days after the blast, at the same time, the doors of all the bunkers opened and a figure emerged from each wearing a radiation protection suit and carrying some equipment that looked like an old TV set top box which they then buried in a shallow grave, presumably to hide it, from what in this barren land? They then retired into their respective bunkers and locked the door. It clearly was some sort of communication system kept in the bunker to avoid damage from the H-EMP pulse. But the bunkers were too well shielded to allow communication with the outside, hence the equipment was brought out as soon as the remaining radiation level allowed people in radiation suits to venture outside for just the five minutes needed. Now the inhabitants of the bunkers could talk to each other and presumably also to those in the space station.

The bunkers had not yet been found and none of the survivors observed this event, they were also too busy staying alive. It was to be years before the survivors had re-established radio communications and discovered the radio traffic between bunkers, proving the existence of pioneers alive in their bunkers.

Although they were not there to record it, there was one more bunker than had been found by Claud and his colleagues. This one was under the rock at Uluru with its entrance buried a few metres away. How did they miss it?

20 NB

Population of Pioneers now 40,000 Population of Survivors now 3 million.

The hunter-gatherers and the townies had long given up their philosophical belief in how the world should move forward in favour of just staying alive. The townies were able to get on with rebuilding as much of the prior age of technology as possible. There were two main problems facing them; they had no teachers, so for example, you could not become a doctor after going to medical school. You could, one supposes, experiment and learn on live patients but no one seemed willing to go that route. There were plenty of books to help but no X-Ray or MRI machines and few surviving drugs and no means of making them. But some persevered and became doctors albeit with limited capabilities.

Of course, the main sickness was still the effects of radiation and the deformities, mutations and diseases that it caused. There was nothing in the textbooks to help them in this respect. The hunter-gatherers proved extremely willing and helpful in the painstaking task of working to re-develop much that had been forgotten in traditional medicines, while they had also developed many treatments of their own based on nature. Between the two groups, 'doctoring' was developing fast without the conflicts between medical science and alternative medicine that was evident in the old world.

The second issue was that most electronic circuit boards had been destroyed by the H-EMP pulse. They were nowhere near being able to remake integrated circuit chips, so the technology at that time was distinctly low-tech. In the old world, it took only 50 years to go from the first transistor to large-scale integrated circuit chips powering computers, and mobile phones and supporting just about every modern technology product. Here, they had the books but not the ability to build what they had read, but they were getting there, slowly. They knew what they were aiming for and how to get there but did not have the means. So, they moved forward slowly, every now and then solving a major problem that had been blocking progress, then spurting forward until they hit the next roadblock.

What they could do was build buildings, they could reclaim bricks, steel, and wood from the rubble as well as make concrete, bricks and steel. They had few machines, and this was hard physical work that very few could do for a whole day. So, the work was divided into four-hour day shifts which practice had shown to be the best way to work. They also took the decision to build for practicality, nothing pretty and designed for no more than a 20-year life. They needed shelter and factory space now, not artwork.

They needed to work step by step; generate electricity, build electro-mechanical devices, rebuild the factories that produced the silicon wafers that were the basis for the production of integrated circuit chips, then use these to build the products. They had good success in creating low-tech factories, but to make silicon wafers they needed state-of-the-art buildings built on rubber foundations to be vibration free, which at that time they couldn't do. However, some other activities were proving to be more successful. Because many of the survivors were miners, they had the knowledge to identify mines and their products and begin to extract coal and oil. They had found badly damaged but to some extent, repairable coal-fired power stations, which previously had been only kept as backup stations but now were generating electricity for their future.

Oil refining had begun using facilities not wholly destroyed and some motors were running; diesel vehicles using only mechanical parts such as mechanical fuel pumps as was the case with some old vehicles. Modern trucks and cars were littered with electronic components which would one day have to be replaced before they would run again. Only veteran cars could be made to run. Yet there were motor vehicles running alongside the current main mode of transport, the horse or its mutated cousin.

One of the main problems for the survivors was geographic spread. They were thinly littered across the world, mainly in small concentrations for safety and at first, they knew nothing about each other, which meant that in many cases the same wheel was being invented in different places, while problems in one place had been overcome in others. Some groups had 're-invented' radio communications but that was of little use until other groups also had a radio. So wireless communication lagged behind physical journeys and meetings, and after a few years when people could think about things other than staying alive, people began to travel and seek each other out, on foot and horse.

When it did happen, the redevelopment radio communications quickly led to the discovery of radio traffic from unknown sources which led to the discovery of bunkers and that there were people living in them. Around the world, the bunkers were discovered, all 19 of them which were assumed to be 20 with one not found yet.

Some survivors had previously discovered or knew about the bunkers before D-Day, while others had found them in the early post-D-Day period, but all had chosen to say nothing about them. Radio at this time was used exclusively for survivor development such as ambulance and aeroplane communication; there was no broadcast radio even for news and no entertainment programmes. This allowed the small group managing radio communications around the world to agree not to broadcast to the bunkers or operate in the fixed frequency band being used by the pioneers or in any way let them know that there were people alive outside the bunkers until such time as a unilateral policy was decided and this would be one of the first jobs for a government which was in the process of being set up.

Once a government had been formed, the existence of the bunkers and pioneers was formally acknowledged. From the radio communications between the bunkers, they knew that there were people alive in the bunkers and that they were the so-called pioneers who had been recruited before D-Day. Some of the survivors knew a little of the story and gradually they pieced together the story of the pioneers and bunkers from scraps of information that different survivors knew.

The clear implication drawn from the discovery of 19 bunkers around the world with people locked in until the radiation was down to a safe level, was that the expectation of the pioneers was that everyone else in the world would be killed. But there were survivors and the new Government decided that the pioneers should be left alone and not be shocked by the existence of survivors. In any event, radiation was still too high for unsuited pioneers to venture out without them going through the same traumas that the pioneers endured. That meant the pioneers would have to stay locked in their bunker dungeons for years more in the full knowledge that there is a new world outside inhabited by millions of people managing to live their lives in the fresh (radioactive) air.

It was also assumed by the Government that the perpetrators of the explosions would have wanted to save themselves and must be among those in the bunkers. So, as and when they emerge, what shall they do with them? They debated long and hard over this question but the longer the bunkers stayed closed the more the debate died away until it stopped altogether. The Government would decide at a later date, or when the bunkers open up. In the meantime, they had other more pressing issues to deal with.

By D-Day plus 18 years the townies had managed to get some veteran airplanes into the air, which in the space of a year had enabled every enclave to have made contact at least with their neighbours. This meant that they could introduce radio communications to each group and by D-Day plus 20, just about the whole survivor world population was in touch via radio. As a result, the pace of change and re-development accelerated greatly. But they kept away from the pioneers internal radio frequencies.

Although there was the start of a high-speed industrial revolution that brought people together, there remained a definite split in ideology between the hunter-gatherers and the townies. The hunter-gatherers took advantage of the start of communications between groups that had been achieved by the townies but wanted nothing to do with moves to get technology back to where it was before D-Day because, in their view, it would inevitably lead once again to nuclear bombs. There was stress among the groups over this, but it stopped short of violence both because they did not want to kill any of the few of them that were left and besides, all had medical problems and were really in no position to fight.

As it turned out, the two groups fitted together very well with the hunter-gatherers taking responsibility for food and water availability, safety from wild animals, which was causing quite a problem in some places, and basic housing. They joined with the townies on schooling and education, news distribution and the spread of good ideas emanating from regional enclaves.

D-Day and its effects on survivors had all but eliminated the power-hungry, the potential despots and the criminal element as every day was a challenge just to stay alive. Thus, the vestiges of civilisation appeared. On a world scale, they formed a single government charged with rebuilding the world, not the same again but a better world. There would be no army but there would be a police force charged with resolving local disputes; larger disputes would be dealt with by the government. The seat of government was located in Antarctica, chosen because it had the lowest radiation levels, the bombs have been in orbit around the equator and Antarctica would not attract old national territorial rivalries, and finally, at that time the weather was not so different as that elsewhere. But it was still very cold there.

Money was created as convenient tokens in just one currency, to represent the value in goods and services supplied. It was effectively based on the original barter currency concept and as such, there would be no value in money as an abstract entity, no profit in trading money and no concept of rich or poor. Money would be a convenient tool for trading.

The teaching of history created much discussion. What did they say about the world before D-Day, the reasons for D-Day and the build-up to it? No one knew the full story or its implications for their future. A history was agreed, steeped in the death and misery that had been caused and impressing the lessons to be learned.

Julie remembered seeing the bunker near her mine and the young pioneers inhabiting it. From her training to mine for Uranium, she knew the half-life of a cobalt adulterated nuclear bomb is 50 years and that it would be 100 years before radiation levels are back to pre-D day levels, although her radiation monitor showed the levels dropping much faster than expected. Nevertheless, there was little incentive to do anything about the bunkers except to tell the next generation and the one after that what to expect and roughly when. However, she had long ago dropped out of attending the countless debates on the subject and was pleased when the government took over responsibility for the bunkers and then quietly dropped the subject.

49 NB

Population of Pioneers now 120,000 Population of Survivors now 20 million.

In the almost fifty years since it happened, society had rebuilt, run by a new generation of children and grandchildren of the original survivors. All the rubble and signs of the blast had gone, as had most of the first round of rebuilding which was replaced with modern, well-designed and in many cases beautiful buildings. Styles were a mixture of the recreation of what was with new and radical designs. They could be and were, proud of their achievements. Electric cars were running on new roads, there were trains and planes and little to tell a stranger what had happened, except perhaps the lack of people. Those that still talked about the bunkers, mused that a pioneer would assume the bombs had failed to detonate although the different architecture and unusual vehicle design would make them think they were in a foreign country.

Most people with obvious radiation damage had died out, but lifespans were still short which meant that people had to grow up more quickly as well as take on senior roles at a younger age.

The new society was a kinder society and there was little crime and violence. Just about all technology-based services were now up and running with a strong emphasis on infrastructure rebuilding and communications development, this time all within a green agenda. People took it for granted that they must be as self-sufficient as possible and at all times work towards sustaining the planet.

It was not Utopia, far from it, radiation and mutations were still serious problems feeding down through the generations. It would be decades before the problem finally disappeared. However, there was no national rivalry, no religious fanaticism, everyone was too busy rebuilding the world.

The one great ongoing discussion centred around why it happened, why was it allowed to happen, was the intention that there should be no survivors other than the pioneers? The general conclusion was that somehow it had been arranged in secret and that only the pioneers were supposed to live through it. So, because there were survivors, killing billions of people, causing decades of suffering, and almost destroying the world, it had all been for nothing.

Book 5
The Aftermath

50 NB

It was 50 years to the day when the doors opened. The scientists among the bunkered groups had noted from the sensors set alongside the communications equipment, that the radiation had reduced to tolerable levels far faster than assumed, which proved to be due to the thriving life around the planet.

A month before the big day, the sleepers in the bunkers were woken up and brought up to speed with the happenings of the last 50 years which was very little as the doors had remained shut and life in the bunkers had gone on largely as planned. The communication facilities hidden outside the bunkers had lasted well and served their purpose. All 20 bunkers had survived as had the space station, a testament to the genius and capability of those who had designed and built the bunkers and space vehicles.

Stored communication equipment, and land and air vehicles were readied and tested, and the long drawn-up plan of action kicked off. They were working on the assumption that there would be much desolation, some mutated plants and a few mutated animals. Since they had been locked away with no means of looking outside, they had no clue that all was not as it seemed, although one or two bunkers had reported noises at the doors as though someone was trying to break in. However, the noises had stopped more than 20 years ago, and it was assumed to be rockfall or another natural phenomenon. More recently, they had detected some interference in their communications facilities which, being locked-in, fixed frequency devices, were unable to be used to investigate the cause.

Peter, now one of the elders of his bunker was very excited at the thought of getting out of the bunker, breathing fresh air seeing the sky and even feeling the rain on his face. Was he remembering it right, it had been so long? He had a month before the doors were opened during which time became a teacher to those born in the bunker. He told them about the world he remembered and about what to expect now. They would all have to work to rebuild the world from scratch. He desperately hoped it would not be as bad as most were assuming.

The survivors had identified 15 locations that looked like bunkers and they had rightly assumed there were more. They had long ago restored radio communications and, over the last few years, had identified the bunker communications facilities and noted that there were 19 bunkers, they identified the location of the other four. But there must be another one, nobody would build 19. Had it failed to survive? They decided not to transmit on the bunker channel and let those inside know what was going on outside, but to listen in and learn about the pioneers as well as those who had created the bunkers and set off the bombs.

They had learnt a lot from listening in to the bunker communications, as well as identifying and locating four of the remaining five bunkers, they had made preparations for the bunkers to open although that could still be many years away. They remained perplexed by the signals which appeared to be coming from the moon. Although they could listen in, this traffic was encrypted and to date, they had not decoded it.

About a month before the doors opened, the communications changed from run-of-the-mill reporting to getting ready to come out. A week before the coming out day, they knew the exact date and time of the exit. They sent a welcome committee to each bunker with an agreed mandate to help them as necessary, bring them up to speed on the events of the last 50 years and generally integrate them into the new world order. One thing was firmly agreed by all survivors, the pioneers were welcome to join and participate in the new society as equals, but they would not be allowed to become rulers, and there would be no weapons allowed, and any found would be destroyed.

The doors of the bunkers opened, and the pioneers came out. The majority of those exiting were born in the bunkers and had never seen the sky, or the sun or felt rain on their faces. Those born before the doors had locked them in for 50 years could hardly remember what fresh air tasted and smelled like. And they kept coming, around 8,000 people from each bunker, men, women and children, the very old who had lived through the 50 years, awake, managing the ecosystem of the bunkers, the first and second generation adults who were born in the bunkers; their young children and lastly, those cryogenically frozen and reawakened. These were people who in their own eyes had woken up the day after D-Day. So many people were locked away in bunkers. The survivors had estimated that there would be less than 100 people per bunker and they were genuinely shocked as they kept coming.

All except the young children looked distinctly unhappy and bewildered, even more so when they saw the reception committee awaiting them. Now it was the time for the pioneers to be shocked and in most cases, angered; had it all been for nothing?

The pioneers regardless of age reacted badly to daylight, the controller had forgotten this and not supplied sunglasses, another mistake. However, the survivors had anticipated it and included sunglasses in a welcome pack for the total number of pioneers they thought were coming out. Additional welcome packs were soon put together, rushed to the bunkers and distributed to the pioneers. Besides sunglasses, the packs contained a short introduction to the basic rules by which the survivors lived, much like the 10 commandments, and a short history starting at the explosion.

One other big surprise was to find their cars and trucks not only redundant but unusable as all transport was electrically powered with fossil fuel burners banned. As they were also soon to find out, helicopters and fixed-wing aircraft were also electrically powered. Survivors really did put the planet first. But the survivors were very grateful for the medications the pioneers brought with them, the books, the games and all other items that they took as run-of-the-mill products. Toilet rolls became a marketable currency.

Of course, the pioneers were taken aback and shocked by the appearance of many survivors, something the survivors themselves had long ago ceased to notice. The pioneers started to show pity but that was soon scotched and once they had had a good look, they too took it in their stride and it ceased to be an issue, just as in the same way survivors and pioneers of all colours got on well together unaware of any differences. Julie and Jacob would have been proud.

The Twentieth Bunker

There was another bunker, the twentieth, a secret bunker not linked by any two-way communications to the other bunkers. It was under the rock at Uluru. In the minutes before the explosion, 10 of the controller's guards had rounded up Chess, Jim and Claud and taken them through a hitherto unknown passage to what was clearly a bunker but a very small one. Waiting for them was the controller, still cloaked and masked.

Without a word they were all tranquilised and put into cryogenic pods along with the 10 guards, being rewarded for their loyalty. The controller switched all systems to automatic and climbed into his freezer pod and all was quiet. The bunker had a signal receiver placed under the Uluru rock, the hope being that it would survive the H-EMP pulse. This would be used to monitor the other bunker communications so that automatic processes could be instituted to wake them up along with the others. If this failed, the bunker was pre-programmed to wake them in exactly 100 years, by when he thought it would be safe.

The receiver had survived, and the wake-up signal was received after just 50 years. The pre-programmed automatic wake-up process started, and they woke up. The controller seemed his normal self, whereas Chess, Jim and Claud were in a state of shock. On checking the bunker's elapsed time monitor, the controller was, however, put out to find that only 50 years had elapsed, had something gone wrong? No, the radiation sensors showed the radiation level to be low and safe for them to exit without radiation suits. They unlocked the door and ventured out intending to set up their full communication antennae, but they were stopped in their tracks by the lush vegetation that faced them instead of the expected barren land or possible sparse scrubland. But the biggest surprise was the gaggle of black faces that appeared before them. Had the explosions failed to happen?

Although they were black and obviously Australian aboriginals, they were fully dressed and spoke to them with well-educated English voices,

"Hello, is this the 20th bunker. The one that we knew existed but could not find anywhere in the world? Is this all of you? Did your communications equipment fail?"

"This is a special bunker," said the controller calmly, "We are the leaders of the pioneers, that is, those who have lived in the bunkers and just come out, and we have been frozen in cryogenic chambers the whole time. Can you tell me if there was an explosion that killed all living things in the world and if so when this happened?" The controller was perplexed, this world was not the one he was expecting.

Calmly and without obvious anger, the aboriginals asked,

"Does this mean you are the ones responsible for almost destroying the world 50 years ago?" The controller nodded.

"Then, you must appear before the World Council which has long had a plan to deal with you as and when you appear. We will escort you part of the way, but first, you will have to remove your mask as the radiation has caused most people to have some variation and we do not judge people based on their differences." The survivors had long got over any embarrassment or singling out. Reluctantly, the controller removed his mask and cloak, and it was clear he had been in a major fire and/or acid attack.

"Thank you. It seems that 10 of you are soldiers or guards and in this world, all weapons are banned, so please give all you have to my colleagues. Also, as guards you are clearly not one of the leaders who blew up the world, so there is no need for you to go to the council, instead, my colleague will take you to the town where you can stay until you decide where you wish to live and what you want to do now you no longer have a job." The controller nodded to the guards in an assuring way and they left with one of the aboriginals.

The remaining four were shepherded to a small coach, similar to those of 50 years ago, but not quite the same. It was electrically powered and almost silent which gave Chess, Jim and Claud the chance to talk. They had been dumbfounded to have tried up to the very last minute to stop the bombs, only to find what seemed to be five minutes later that they were 50 years into the future alongside the controller and being taken as part of the bomber group. They had said nothing until now as their wits returned to them. At last, Chess cleared his throat and spoke, his voice not working very well for his first two sentences but after being given a drink of water, his normal authoritative voice returned,

"My name is Chester Chessington, everyone calls me Chess, this is Jim Bray and my other colleague is Claud Liphook. We are not part of this gentleman's bomb plot, indeed we tried very hard to stop it and we clearly failed. It would seem that we were drugged and hijacked and put into freezers in his bunker." He paused, he had not called Jim, General Jim Bray, since there were no weapons, there could not be an army, so calling him a general might not go down too well. Chess was very confused, he did not know whether to be grateful or not but here they were, alive 50 years later, not a day older and all thanks to the controller. Claud explained his expertise and interests, he had two big questions,

"Why are they alive and how did the planet recover so quickly?" Joe, the most knowledgeable of the aboriginals on the subject explained,

"The bombs were clearly meant to destroy the whole planet but some survived, about one million across the world, having been in mines or otherwise screened from the blast and radiation. Life was bad after that with most dying quickly and with great disfigurement and mutations. They realised the only solution was to live with it and have children quickly in the hope the generations would either adapt to accept a radiated world or live long enough for the radiation to drop to a low level." He paused and then continued.

"Both have been the case, and now the population is about 20 million and the radiation all but gone." He paused again as if to allow the group to absorb what was being told to them,

"As far as the planet is concerned, without billions of humans to pollute the earth, rivers and air, it soon recovered using the radiation to mutate into faster growing plants and animals. In turn, this dissipated the radiation such that what should have taken 100 years, actually took just 50 years." Claud was now grinning as big a grin as he could make. And it was so fitting that an aboriginal was telling this story. Joe continued, obviously delighting in the look of glee on Claud's face and confusion on the faces of Chess and Jim. The controller was not capable of showing facial expressions,

"In those 50 years civilisation has recovered, technology recreated, and people's lifestyles are not dissimilar to those of 50 years ago. Fossil fuels had been essential in the early years but were banned now, as was anything nuclear. Today's world is electrically powered." The others in the welcoming committee explained that there are now more aboriginals in Australia than those of European extract, the aboriginal culture more quickly adapting to the need for a ground-up approach, living off the land, not needing concrete buildings or motor cars. Proudly they explained that they were all equal now, across all nations in the world.

They arrived at an airfield with just one airplane on it, propellors idling and looking ready for take-off, just what Chess and the others would have expected 50 years ago, but the plane's engines were idling silently, and it was clearly also electrically powered. Once they were in, the aboriginals said goodbye and they were on their own with the pilot who was not talkative. The flight took about an hour during which they were mainly silent spending their time looking out the windows at the lush vegetation in place of what used to be desert scrubland. They landed at a larger airport in what they found out had been Alice Springs. No sooner had they landed than they were shepherded onto a much larger airplane which took off without delay.

The plane was almost empty and most of the seats had been removed to create an office in which the four of them were motioned to take seats at a board room type table by the three other occupants. The four had a sense of foreboding but the three were polite and friendly and were the first to clear the air,

"We are senators in the Council and we are going to Antarctica which is where the seat of Government is housed." Claud jumped in with a comment,

"Besides being the least irradiated since the satellites carrying the bombs were put in orbit around the equator, the seat of government should be in what was neutral territory." The three senators nodded.

The three 'survivors' brought the group up to speed with the happenings of the last 50 years which all but the controller marvelled at. He could not understand how anyone could have survived. It had to be the doing of Professor Wu Lee,

I should not have let Serrano hurt him, he thought. Nevertheless, the prime aim of the controller had been achieved and the world 're-started', but he could have achieved it without the pioneers, or so it appeared.

Chess acted as spokesman for his group and told the whole story from beginning to end with interruptions from Jim and Claud as and when they felt it necessary, the controller stayed silent – thinking. When Chess had finished, the three senators came over to the controller and shook his hand recognising the genius that made all this happen. Chess and the others, were shocked, this man has created the biggest genocide ever and they shook his hand. The controller saw his opportunity and said,

"Gentlemen, thank you for this. I will not bother with my reasons for what I did, instead I would like to offer you my technology, especially nuclear fusion which has kept us alive this past 50 years."

Now it was the turn of the senators to look shocked. One said without considering the opportunities,

"Anything nuclear is banned, we do not want another world calamity at any time in our future. We have destroyed all vestiges of nuclear technology including documentation and training courses. As we speak, your bunkers are being stripped of their fusion power sources." However, the controller was not downhearted, he had another trick up his sleeve.

They were given new clothing, appropriate to the Antarctic weather and quickly taken into the government building complex part of which was a hotel. They were each given a room, further changes of clothing for indoor use, a room service food menu and a telephone number to call if they needed anything. Chess asked about payment and offered his AMEX card hardly expecting it to work after 50 years but in any event, it was waved away with the comment.

"You don't need money here." They were given 12 hours to sleep or do whatever they liked. They would not be locked in, and they could go to each other's rooms or explore the complex. They all thought they would explore this wonderful place and find out about the seat of Government but instead, they all quickly fell fast asleep, their first proper sleep in 50 years and had to be woken up after 12 hours.

Two hours later they sat in front of a tribunal called specifically to deal with the pioneer situation and now to include the perpetrator of the genocide. They had found the bunkers years ago and had long prepared for this meeting. They had clearly been listening in to the talks in the plane bringing them to Antarctica, so a great deal of repetition was avoided.

"Just a few questions to fill us in," stated the chairman of the panel, "We knew there was something in space, but could not see it or decode its transmissions. Can you tell us about it, presumably it is also of your doing?" The controller filled them in and played his first 'joker'.

"In case the bunkers did not survive, I built a space station behind the moon and populated it with pioneers who occupied the spare space in the 15 rockets carrying the bombs. After depositing the bombs in orbit around the earth, the rockets took the pioneers, 2,000 in total, to the space station where they have lived for the past 50 years," Then came the second 'joker'.

"The rockets will return to Earth shortly but even allowing for the extra space in the rockets now travelling without bombs, there will not be enough room for the whole expanded complement of men, women and children. So, the rocket will have to return to pick up the rest of the pioneers, but there is no launch pad now on Earth. In addition, the space station is a wonderful research facility which I hope you will allow to continue, so we will need ongoing two-way travel. Will you allow me to construct a launchpad on Earth and use it to create a shuttle to the space station?"

The tribunal duly noted this request and asked a few more detailed questions about the whole plan and its execution and then went into recess for discussions among themselves. After just an hour they reconvened. The leader of the tribunal made a statement.

"There are four matters I will deal with. However, this is a new situation and nothing I say here and now is cast in concrete, we are an open and democratic society. Firstly, I want to deal with the planet and its inhabitants. Although we are only 20 million people, we are spread over the whole planet and the different cultures of old are showing themselves again. We do not know enough about them or their previous lifestyles. Claud Liphook, you have the skills we lack, and we

would like you to lead a team to travel the world and ensure everyone is dealt with fairly according to their traditions.

Second, we need to deal with the pioneers. We believe they have many of the skills we need, and we would like to bring them into our society without any status difference. However, we know it will take time to assimilate them, especially as we are seeing a great deal of disillusion among your pioneers. Chester Chessington and Jim Bray, your military history means you are good organisers, and we would like you to look after the integration of the pioneers including relevant knowledge transfer, for example among doctors.

Third, the spaceships. Of course, we will help build the rocket launchers to allow all on the space station to be rescued. We also support the establishment of a permanent research facility there. The problem is the use of nuclear fusion to power the rockets and the space station. We have decided to allow its use to remain in place to meet just these two special requirements for which there is no alternative but with all knowledge kept only at the space station and with research at the facility to include pursuing other technologies to replace nuclear fusion." The controller smiled as far as his deformities allowed.

"Finally, what to do about the controller. We have decided he should move permanently to the space station in order to keep his knowledge of nuclear fusion off the planet, to allow him to research alternatives and to head up all the other research being carried out there."

Only one of the four was entirely happy. The controller felt he had been let off lightly and was free to carry on his mission, albeit not on Earth but on the other hand, that could be an advantage in that it would give him the freedom to do as he chose. The other three loved their appointments but were deeply concerned about the controller being given free reign at the space station. Surely, he must pay more than that and must be controlled. Both Chess and Jim independently decided they would kill him the moment he steps out of line, but they said nothing.

Pioneers

The great surprise for all pioneers was to find a population living outside the bunkers and whose achievements could only be marvelled at. At the start of their 'liberation', the pioneers' reactions to finding people on the outside were predictable; shock is the only word that can describe the feelings of the pioneers who had lived through the whole 50 years when they realised their ordeal had been for nothing. Those pioneers who had been frozen, woke up and felt and looked as though just one day had passed since the explosion; they were still young and eager and were yet to absorb the enormity of being shut in a bunker needlessly. The feelings of those born in the bunkers were of wonderment when they saw the sky, the sun and the grass-covered landscape. They were yet to appreciate what they had missed although the older ones now in their late 40s were the first among this group to feel cheated of a normal life. However, one look at the survivors told the pioneers that the alternative of living through radiation must have been terrible.

Given the imperative to procreate while ensuring the gene pool was as mixed as it could be, the swapping of partners, needed little encouragement at first, but later had become a ritual and it was no surprise to find that while all the sexual variations were tried out without restriction or judgement, they died out and in general, heterosexual activity became the norm and one-to-one partnerships began to be formed that later became formal marriages. Nevertheless, once in a while, changes occurred for a night or two, including a switch of partner gender without rancour from any of the participants, just like taking a holiday or going to a dinner party with friends. The growth of the pioneer population had been much faster than the controller had allowed for and it was lucky they did not have to stay in their bunkers for 100 years. It had taken Peter only a year to find a long-term partner and start a family.

There were the grandchildren and great-grandchildren who were excited about seeing the world they had been denied for their whole lives. It did not matter that there were people living outside their bunker, they would have new friends to play with. And there were the children in the other bunkers to whom they had talked but never met. The older children began to question their teachers, the elders who had taught them to expect desolation and destruction, and that they were the only humans still alive. Nevertheless, they were quick to accept it and begin to integrate with these people, the survivors as they proudly referred to themselves.

Soon after the initial contact when the bunker doors opened, reality sank into those who had been frozen that everyone they had ever known was dead and they were newcomers in a new world. How would they integrate into a different and somewhat alien world? Freezing and unfreezing were new technologies and the effect on the body was unknown. So, here was another risk the controller had taken including on himself. Of the 2,000 people frozen, six claimed they had been awake and paralysed the whole time. All were in a sorry state with 4 committing suicide at the earliest time. The other two appeared to respond to treatment mainly from Peter, but within weeks they had got into fights with pioneers who had stayed awake. One was killed by his opponent, the other went into a catatonic trance and remained there. It is not known whether or not he was awake while in the catatonic state. He never recovered.

Most of the ones who had stayed awake and their first-generation children, all of whom were approaching 50 years of age, were distinctly unhappy and integration would prove to be particularly difficult for them. They had been duped into staying in the bunkers for 50 years when at recruitment, they were told it would be for one year and now that they found people on the outside were alive and well and the planet recovered and rebuilt, they felt their lives had been wasted. It had been twice as bad as a life sentence for murder. Nelson Mandela had served little more than half their time. Added to this was the knowledge that everyone they were related to or just known, was dead. They would also be alone in this new world.

In the bunkers during the 50 years, although most managed to appear normal and go through their daily lives, without unduly drawing attention to themselves, the boredom, monotony and the restricted company were really beginning to affect them. There was no way they would have kept their sanity for 100 years. There had been a spate of suicide attempts in a few of the bunkers but in all cases, the person had been revived, in a few cases multiple times and in the end, the people gave up and settled down again, if you could call it that. A few others had gone "stir crazy" and become violent, destroying things, not people. It was assumed they wanted to damage the bunker such that it would have to open the outer door. These people could not be allowed to remain as they were and were taken to the hospital area to be drugged up and 're-trained'. When they reappeared, they were like living shells of people, best described in the book 1984.

Those on the space station followed a similar pattern of feelings and behaviour but with two significant extra factors to consider. They knew the rocket launch gantries had been destroyed and that the first rocket trip taking people home would be the last, at least for a long time. Who would stay and who would go? Secondly, the space station had become a significant scientific research centre. The scientists wanted to stay and continue the work, but they were running out of equipment and testing capability. They needed the rockets to come back.

Peter was coming up to his 75th birthday and he felt his age as he wandered around outside the bunker. At first, he met with universal dislike and anger from the survivors, but Peter had organised trips into the bunker for the survivors which included a history presentation of the lives of the pioneers from the explosion to the present day. The more he talked with survivors, the more he realised that life had been no picnic for them, as well as suffering from radiation poisoning, they had to rebuild from scratch with no heavy equipment to help them.

The pioneer's stores included tents and prefabricated buildings each of which could double as a light engineering factory or a dwelling for four families. The survivors had also built some basic living accommodations for those pioneers they had assumed would be alive and well when they came out of the bunkers. Finally, some had decided to stay in their bunker apartments. The pioneers were told that in this world money was not an issue and that it was used merely to keep account of the use of resources available from one and used by another. For the present, they had free use of money and they were left for the first months to get their lives together and find their place in modern society. In the first year of his time in the bunker, Peter had married and soon three children were born to him and his wife. At that time, he was still a 'gung-ho' pioneer despite the fact that what he supposed would be one year had turned into 100 years. Now he was only grateful it had been just 50 years and he was still alive to witness the new world.

Peter was an obvious leader and being a (trainee) doctor, had much sought-after knowledge. He was given a job at a nearby hospital as a knowledge exchange consultant and re-housed nearby. Only his youngest child joined them, the other two had their own lives and families to look after. There had been some problems in pioneers adjusting, as well as a number of rivalries becoming evident. Peter, being an 'elder', set up a local community liaison and help centre and problems were soon dissipated. However, there was one problem that would not go away, and that was the banning of all things nuclear, which everyone understood but meant that the bunker fusion power source was shut down and dismantled. Alternative power was supplied but it could hardly keep up with the demands for power in the bunker and eventually, the bunkers were abandoned. They had served their purpose.

The means of travel brought by the pioneers were also unusable as they used fossil fuel which was banned. In the case of road and rail transport, most of what was brought along in the bunker was repurposed and retrofitted with electric motors, while the helicopters and light aircraft were deemed not suitable for conversion and stripped for parts.

Health in the bunkers had been physically good during the 50-year lockdown, there was no 'flu, no measles, no chicken pox, etc. Cancer was rare and generally cured and genetic diseases had been bred out of the bunker population. On the other hand, although the radiation had affected every survivor to some extent, the survivors had also suffered from all the same diseases as were prevalent in the 20th Century.

It was an unfortunate side effect of having two populations living apart for 50 years, in that the pioneers soon after coming out of their bunkers, started getting ill with all those diseases easily coped with by the survivors such as measles and chickenpox. Those born during the 50-year lockdown in their bunkers were particularly susceptible and many died.

Peter knew about all the diseases that were rampant among the pioneers and made good use of the antibiotics carried in the bunkers, as well as advising the nascent drug industry on the different medications and their uses. Nevertheless, it was a difficult period for the pioneer families.

Although a major problem for the pioneers, the physical illnesses were well understood. The same could not be said for mental illness. During their time locked into the bunkers, mental illness seemed to be present to a limited extent and manageable. Everyone had a role to play and was kept busy, there was no time for mental illness. However, once the bunkers were opened, it was a different story and it soon became apparent that rather than having a limited problem while the pioneers were locked in the bunkers, the problem was a major one that came to the surface as soon as they exited the bunkers.

Those staying awake felt cheated of their lives, they had stayed, cocooned in their bunker for 50 years unnecessarily as it turned out. Everyone they had ever known was dead, 'The best years of their life' had been lost, all for nothing. They had been lied to and cheated and the sad thing was, there was nothing they could do about it. They went in as young, eager pioneers and have come out as old men and women.

Those born in the bunkers could not come to terms with what the real world was like when their world was the cocoon of the bunker, while those frozen could not get used to the new order in the world. They wanted what they had had, the pursuance of wealth and power, the feeling of seniority over others; a return to the 'normal' as was and not the 'new normal' of today.

Peter became a leading expert in the treatment of mental illness, however, there were no easy answers. If the whole thing had been one giant experiment for the controller, it might well have been called a success at the technical level, although the presence of survivors would call that claim into question, but on a personal level, it had failed and badly. Peter had to spend the rest of his life putting broken minds back together again.

Volvo P1800

Three years after coming out of his bunker, Peter, now 78 years old, had his first opportunity to go back to his old home, that is, to the map reference that was once Copenhagen. It had been a city sitting on the coastal islands of Zealand and Amager with a bridge linking it to southern Sweden. Although he had prepared himself for shock and disappointment, he nevertheless had his breath taken away by what he saw.

There was no devastation only a new city, still called Copenhagen, although as was current practice, the word New was placed in front of the reuse of existing names. New Copenhagen was a rebuilt modern city, reminiscent of some aspects of the old city but with no recognisable streets or buildings. In fact, the bomb had changed the local geography, making new waterways and filling in others. The bridge to Malmo in Sweden was of course gone. This made it extremely difficult for him to get to the exact location of his house, but he eventually arrived there and saw a new build house in place of his home of 50 odd years ago. Although he knew this would be the case, he was visibly moved, and tears came to his eyes.

He knocked at the door hoping that he might find some rapport with the new owner. A man of about 30 answered the door, clearly affected by radiation,

"Hello, can I help you," said the man. By now the survivors and pioneers had integrated to a position where you could not tell at a first glance whether the person was one or the other. However, an elderly man at the door with no obvious deformities was clearly a 'stay awake' pioneer. So, he was not surprised to hear Peter say,

"My name is Peter and I am one of the pioneers who stayed awake from the explosion through to today. Before the explosion, my house stood here and I wanted to see it again before I die. I hope you don't mind," replied Peter. The man's eyes opened wide and he responded,

"Come in, come in. My name is Max Peterson and this is my wife Julia and my children Peter and Marie." After they sat down had tea and cakes and chatted over matters of mutual interest, came the big surprise, Max smiled and began,

"This is our second house on this site, the first being simple and quick to erect as we needed a home. Later I built this house together with my friends. We all help each other to rebuild and improve our lives. But I digress, when clearing the land for the first house, I came across parts of a car that was already in pieces when the bomb struck, some parts were in labelled bags, others were strewn around. Being a survivor's son, I had no opportunity to drive or learn anything about the mechanics of cars, we were just trying to stay alive and rebuild our world. So I know precious little about cars, especially how to put one together, but I felt this car, if I could rebuild it, would provide a link to my father and his father who lived before the explosion," Max paused and Peter jumped for joy,

"Was there anything to say what type of card it was?" Max went over to his desk, opened a drawer and pulled out something silver and shiny. It was the tailgate badge of the car and it read 'Volvo P1800'. Peter could not contain himself and he almost shouted,

"It is my car, my pride and joy in the old world. It was in pieces because I got drunk and crashed it. What are you doing with it? Have you started rebuilding it?"

"I would not know where to start and had planned to do some research and self-education first," said Max, "would you like to see the pieces?" There was no stopping Peter and soon they were in Max's garage/shed where he had assembled the parts.

Peter quickly judged that most of the parts were there plus some that did not belong to the P1800. The engine was in one piece, but the chassis was clearly bent, probably just from the accident, and the body shell was in a bad state having been hit by falling masonry in the explosion. Peter judged he could fix it with a lot of welding and new metal. However, all the glass was gone which he judged would be irreplaceable.

Back in the house, Max offered the remains of the car to Peter.

"Peter, I have never seen a grown man so happy. The car is yours," but Peter made a counteroffer,

"The car is yours, on this site where it belongs. With your permission, I will come regularly to work with you rebuilding the car, while at the same time teaching you the skills needed and the mechanics of motor cars of old," all agreed and Peter became a frequent visitor over the ensuing years. The car was finished, complete with glass, but the week before Peter came on his next trip, eager and knowing the car was finished, Peter died. He never had the chance to drive it again. but the Volvo P1800, having been rebuilt 3 times was proudly used by Max (with a fossil fuel dispensation) until it was retired to a museum some years later, the car then being 127 years old.

Perhaps that drunken accident was providence taking a hand in making Peter decide to become a pioneer and remain with it even though he had serious doubts, which were subsequently proven to be correct.

Survivors

Julie and Jacob had lived a full life, surviving longer than most other survivors, probably because they had lived 1.5 km down a mine during the early days avoiding the high radiation prevalent everywhere else. This statement of achievement hides the pain and heartache they went through for 50 long years. The decrease in radiation over time was not matched by an improvement in their health as the cumulative effect of exposure to radiation took its toll on their bodies. But they did not give up. They were determined to play their part to the full in the rebuilding of their world.

The bombs had not caused a continental shift and all the people they met in the first 20 years were South African and generally supported apartheid, even the black and coloured arrivals. Julie and Jacob were having none of it and the new arrivals either adjusted and ignored colour and racial differences or they were sent on their way; cruel but necessary. Of course, the high mixed-race birth rate and the effects of radiation soon made it almost impossible to tell the ethnic origination of anyone.

So, when the bunkers opened up, Julie and Jacob were still alive, just. They were both invalids and were being looked after by their children. Yes, these two racially different people, brought up in an atmosphere of hate, had supported each other, and on many occasions, saved each other's lives, and finally had come together and lived the rest of their lives as a married couple. They had had five children, but one had died of its deformities leaving four, all of whom had participated fully in the rebuilding of their planet, despite their deformities and mutations. They now had 10 grandchildren, the family doing its part to re-populate the earth. None of the grandchildren showed any sign of mutation or deformity, recovery had been much faster than anyone could have hoped for.

Like other survivors, when the South African bunker opened and the pioneers appeared, initial fears and dislikes were soon overcome when they realised that the pioneers were just 'foot soldiers' who had been duped into thinking they would be in hibernation for just one year when those in charge had intended 100 years. The perpetrators of this heinous crime were not in this bunker. Resentment turned to pride when the pioneers marvelled at what had been achieved in 50 years and in an environment of high radiation.

Coal had been mined in the early days to supply much-needed heat and energy. with Julie and Jacob knowing about mining methods and practices especially at the Kloof mine, directing the work. They had been given the authority and they reorganised the mine's function and reopened it, although they were not fit enough to actually do their old jobs. The Kloof mine had been a gold and uranium mine but Julie knew when the lower levels of the mine were dug, several coal seams had been passed and ignored. She supervised the change of function into a coal mine which provided the much-needed coal-based energy the rebuilding of the planet needed.

However, fossil fuels had now been banned and the mine had been permanently closed. They had stripped out all the usable and useful equipment and exploded the mine shafts creating a fitting tomb for all those miners and others who were buried in the mine. The uranium was left there, and the gold was mostly left there. They had mined a ton of gold for use in the electronics industry. Jewellery was little used and there was no such thing as a gold-backed currency, so there was no other use for gold. Few, if any, besides Julie and Jacob knew of the gold and the uranium in the mine, so when it was closed, they felt there would be no reason ever to reopen it.

Shaun

Shaun had heard of the bunkers but never lived to see them opening; perhaps given the hardship he had suffered during the early years this was a good thing. What Shaun could never understand is why the earth had not been completely destroyed with no survivors. What was the point of leaving some alive unless it was a test of humankind's ability to survive? But who would want to do this, who would have the resources and why wasn't he stopped? And in that case, why did they need pioneers? As with all people given difficulties to overcome, such as caring for sick people or undertaking risky tasks, Shaun had become a better person as a result of the bomb and its aftermath, not that such a consideration is any justification for what happened.

Shaun had neither the appetite nor the capability to go drinking, hoaring and fighting as of old. What strength he had gone into rebuilding the world. However, when he was not working, he enjoyed telling stories 'around the campfire'. He often talked of the pub across the road from the hospital as being where he would drink before the bombs, and which pointed him to the life-saving hospital when the bombs came. When the rebuilding was well underway, his friends one night blind folded him and took him for a walk. When they removed the blindfold, he found he was back in his pub rebuilt as close as they could to its original style. He did no more hoaring or fighting but he enjoyed the odd drink or two.

The Controller

The controller had set himself up as the leader of the space station, a facility wholly dedicated to science. All those who were not scientists or their families were sent back to earth. There was now a regular shuttle between the space station and Earth using fusion-powered spacecraft, a concession made only because there was no alternative. Very little was known about what was being researched at the space station and visiting scientists gained the impression that what they saw was only a fraction of what was going on there.

The controller had taken to wearing his mask and cloak again, more to impress others than for any other reason. After all, everyone remembers Darth Vader. All his closed-door research was based on fusion technology as he needed the vast amounts of power it can produce. His first task was to find some way of hiding it, that is, put a 'wrapper' around it which can make full use of the fusion power but present it as being a different type of power source, for example, Hydrogen based.

Once achieved, he could develop a new long-range weapon, to fight off alien attacks he would say if challenged, but he never was challenged and now the weapon was pointing at Earth. He would have his revenge.

Chess and Jim often talked about the controller and what was going on in the space station. The lack of firm information about all of what was going on made them certain the controller was up to no good. They would have to do what they both knew had to be done. Who should do it?

"It must be me," said Chess firmly, "I killed an innocent man in Helsinki, and I failed to stop the explosion."

"Nonsense," replied Jim, "You tried harder than anyone and you nearly did it. The problem all along was that the plan was already in place and in motion, we were both too late from the very start. It must be me since I worked for them through STP Industries and failed to spot what was going on, as well as letting Serrano kill and maim countless people." They continued to argue and got nowhere. They thought of playing cards and leaving it to an unknown mix of chance and skill, but they realised the stronger cardplayer, Jim would always win. In any event, Jim won the day when he played his Joker. He reached into his pocket and pulled out a letter dated four weeks before the explosion and said,

"I did not want to give this to you and have it affect our work in trying to stop the bombs back then or now, in helping rebuild the world. It says I have incurable cancer and have only months to live. The 50-year delay has had no effect, I still have only a few months to live. So, it must be me—" Chess tried to reply but the words would not come out, instead tears came rolling down his cheek. It had to be Jim! They both got very drunk that night.

Chess and Jim hijacked the next shuttle being readied to go to the space station, taking off all passengers and substituting Jim masquerading as one of the scientists due to visit the space station. Jim had kept his handgun as a souvenir, illegally of course. They said their goodbyes, both in tears and Chess got off the shuttle and watched its departure. One thing he was certain of, Jim would not be coming back, succeed or fail; and in the latter case, Chess would carry out the execution.

But he need not have feared. The rocket docked and as soon as the doors opened, the controller saw Jim on his view screen and immediately screamed,

"What is he doing here? Before he can have time to cause any trouble, dismiss the welcoming committee and bring him straight to me." Why was he here? Had his subterfuge been found out? The door opened and Jim entered. Without a word, Jim pulled out the gun and fired five times at the controller, almost an echo of Chess's actions in Helsinki but this time the right man died. He walked over to the body, and took off the mask to make sure it really was the controller and to make sure he was dead. He put the gun to his head and fired the 6th bullet.

Chess Chessington

Chess did not know how he should be feeling. He empathised with the survivors, admired their achievements, and felt guilty that he had not been with them. But here he was 50 years later and not a day older, it was his $50^{th}/100^{th}$ birthday. He was extremely pleased with the jobs given to him and Jim as he enjoyed working with him and looked forward to what, he was sure, would prove to be a most rewarding role. He had found a reason to justify his presence in this new world, and it was a new world, he could just as easily have been on a different planet.

Everyone he knew was dead, his family, the Weasel, Tam and now Jim. Claud was still there but he was busily ensconced flying around the world encouraging the restart of ethnic communities and reawakening the diversity of humankind, this time without generating religious fanaticism.

He reflected on what had happened, trying to work out the why. He had some of the pieces but not all, in fact, he did not even know the controller's real name, so he continued to think of him as the controller. It all went back to the make-up of STP Industries first board.

He regarded Michael Kowelski purely as an unknowing frontman and stooge. Nothing of interest here.

Sir James Scott had distanced himself as soon as his first pay cheque arrived and was clearly there just to put his name on the letterhead. Nothing of interest here.

He did not know that the controller had been badly beaten and given life-changing injuries by Serrano and that this was the trigger that led to the creation of the controller and his plan to destroy the world. So, why was Serrano on the board? He did not know for certain who killed Serrano, but his strong suspicion was that it was Tony Silbeck as there was a rumour that Tony had suffered at the hands of Serrano.

He did not know that Sergei Bucholova had hired Serrano to teach Joe aka the controller a lesson. Sergei had been shocked at the damage done by Serrano to Joe. It was not what he had intended as the man was clearly no longer fit enough to carry on his trading activities. Chess assumed that Sergei was there purely for financial reasons and he did not know that Sergei's action in hiring Serrano to teach the controller a lesson started the chain of events that almost killed the world.

He was certain that Tony Silbeck was Rhino and that the controller had needed someone with his talents to achieve his ends, hiding them from Chess and others as well as setting false clues and trails. He was also sure that Tony Silbeck had killed Serrano.

And he was equally sure that Raymond Carver had been recruited to run the production of the secret rockets, gantries and other necessities. This explained why Carver was ostensibly second in command of production. But he did not think that Carver was party to the grand plan. If anything, he would have assumed that the plan was to start WW3.

He knew why Professor Wu Lee had joined STP Industries and although he was appalled that Wu Lee had made the bombs that almost destroyed the earth, he believed that he also had to thank him for reducing the payload of the bombs which had saved the world from total annihilation, at least that is what the controller had said when he found out that there were survivors. In addition, it was the invention of the safe fusion reaction which kept the pioneers alive for 50 years and opened up the way for space travel and exploration.

Jim Bray and Claud Liphook had already explained their presence on the STP Industries board.

Since Chess was not aware of the hand that Sergei Bucholova and Vito Serrano in forging the creation of the controller, his reflections left him none the wiser and he would spend the rest of his life wondering, although he was pretty certain it had something to do with the injuries he had sustained. One does not get permanent life-changing injuries like those without also getting some degree of mental scarring.

Chess decided to write down all he actually did know in a book to inform people who in general did not know much besides that part that directly affected them.

In writing his book Chess time and again came upon his actions and questioned whether he had taken the right decisions and whether, if he had acted differently, he could have stopped it. It was quite clear now that he had been used all along. He would be the front man seeking answers and being given a false trail to hide the real events and actions. He had killed an innocent man thinking he was the controller. He had assumed his people had decommissioned the control centre which, in point of fact was a dummy.

In the end, he knew he, Jim Bray and Claud Liphook had done their best and there was never a chance that they could stop it, except by bombing the rockets and killing thousands of innocent pioneers. He was equally sure that the controller had arranged it such that if one bomb hit one rocket, they would all explode. The effect on the earth of such a large explosion in one place would most likely split the earth and destroy it as a planet which was not what the controller wanted but what he had to do in the event of his plan being thwarted.

Chess and Jim had been given a job to do by the new Government and now there was just Chess. Months later, Chess found out that Jim's condition was operable, and that Jim had sacrificed his life for Chess.

Throughout this time, a thought had been floating around at the back of his mind; one that scared him. It started off as a mind-wandering conjecture, like the thoughts you have when you are not quite fully asleep, and your dreams are linked to your conscious thoughts. If given the choice, and knowing that the destruction of all living things on the earth was about to take place, what choice would he make? His conscience said to be a survivor, but the easiest and possibly most exciting would be to be cryogenically frozen and wake up after 50 years so that he could witness and participate in the new world. He was not the sort of person to commit suicide and he saw no point in being an awake pioneer if there are also survivors. He judged that as the worst option. In the end, all this taught him was to be thankful he was frozen even though it was at the hand of the person responsible for destroying the world.

Which is where Chess began to have other thoughts that turned into nightly nightmares. A pioneer doctor called Peter helped him through this period and the thoughts faded over time. What were they? Knowing of the growing problems the world was having some 50 years ago and the world as it is today, was the controller right to do what he did, was he the saviour of humankind? If Chess was put in the same position would he do the same? Night after night Chess stood in front of that big red button trying to stop himself from pressing it and night after night he fell asleep not knowing what he would have done.

Claud Liphook was eternally grateful for the job he had been given by the new Government and even thought well of the controller (some aspects only) which had resulted in him being healthy and in the prime of his life in 50 NB. He loved the work and described himself as a missionary, given the authority and job of developing cultural diversity based on the old ways and religions, not converting anyone, just re-awakening their heritage. At the same time, he evangelised the needs of the planet and how it worked in harmony with humankind.

The world must not be put in danger again by the actions of men and women.

Claud Liphook was a believer in the Gaia mythology and wondered whether the world was the prime mover in acting to save itself, but no use trying to convince others as he could find no tangible evidence that would convince his peers. But what drove the controller to move from being the Caped Crusader, killing in ones, to one committing mass murder killing in billions, and becoming the controller? What drove Professor Wu Lee to adjust the bombs' power to ensure that there were some human survivors left to repopulate the world in harmony rather than competition?

Claud Liphook was Chess's saviour; he was a frequent but short stay visitor to Chess who had confided his fears in Claud who saw things differently. He was excited by the richness of culture and ethnic pride that he was uncovering and supporting, all without the jealousies and fanaticism of old. People were developing pride in their cultural heritage and so long as it continued, the diversity being developed will ensure attempts at dictatorial action will come to nought. His view of Chess's problem was that he should accept what has happened and rejoice in the better world created.

However, Claud's most telling argument was why had he, Claud, been frozen for 50 years, end up healthy and in the prime of his life in 50 NB? Not only that, he had been given what he classed as the best job in the world, working to bring back the planet and its inhabitants to its former glory and then move forward, humankind in harmony with the planet, to the betterment of all. It must be pre-ordained; it must be Gaia.

100 NB

If this was all an experiment, a very big experiment, and one that failed in that there were survivors as well as pioneers, it can be viewed at two levels, 50 NB and 100 NB. In the case of 50 NB, the experiment was about the human spirit, their determination to stay alive and overcome the greatest adversities. In the case of 100 NB, it is about human nature. Will humankind and the world it lives in revert back to what it was prior to D-Day, renewal of the fight for wealth and power; the superiority of one group over another, be it hair colour, height, skin colour, ethnicity, it does not matter what.

We are at least 105 years away from 100 NB and therefore do not know. What is highly likely, if not certain, is that the world will be in one of two states, completely destroyed or in very good shape. Today's sick world will not exist. Humans will go on from 50 NB and develop a better fitter world but at some point, humans will be given choices, continue to live as one with the planet and keep it healthy or live a more 'comfortable' life but in so doing damage the planet just a little. For example, cumulative overfishing leading to the extinction of many fish species, with a knock-on effect on the whole food chain. Depleting the earth's resources and then dumping the waste when the products produced are no longer needed instead of re-cycling. And so on, a little bit at a time until the tipping point is reached, and the earth is destroyed.

Today at D-Day minus X years, where X is between 10 and 50, we cannot know what the future will hold, only that the signs are not good. The controller had a mission to root out injustice and those that would hurt others as he had been hurt. He had come to the conclusion that humankind was beyond redemption, vigilantes fighting individual criminals could not succeed, and neither could police forces fighting national battles, or armies fighting international battles. This brought him to the inevitable conclusion he arrived at.

Chester Chessington may not have found out why the controller had done what he did, but the death of the controller was not quite the end of the story; he had the last laugh up his sleeve, perhaps that is not the correct impression to give, and it is better to call it an explanation and justification as he saw it. The controller had assumed that it would be 100 years before they all left the bunkers and that they would be just coming out to a world devoid of people with only the pioneers surviving. However, he recognised that not all of the bunkers would survive and that his bunker could well be one of the failing bunkers. It was his plan to take control of the pioneers, a leader, a *de facto* god when they came out, so what would happen if the controller was not there? He had to make provision for that eventuality,

The bunkers had long ago been destroyed but one had been replicated in the Peace Museum, which tracked the world over the last 100 years and held many artifacts and pictures of those times. The museum bunker was much smaller than a real bunker but had been properly fitted out with items taken from a real bunker as it was being dismantled. Close to the entrance to the bunker was a prize exhibit, a fully restored and working Volvo P1800 petrol-driven motor car.

It was exactly 100 years since the bombs went off and something was happening in the museum bunker. Somewhere in the old electronics, a timer went off and a video started up. It showed the controller in cape and mask speaking to what he thought were newly liberated pioneers. It was 7 p.m. in the evening in the museum and the only ones present were the museum cleaning staff. They called the museum curator who replayed the video and took it straight to the Government, the centre of which was still in Antarctica.

The Government emergency cabinet was immediately called into session to discuss the video. It contained the controller's account of the events leading up to the bombing, his justification for doing it and structure for a new government to be led by him if he was still alive. The description of events given by the controller before, during and after the bombs went off and his expectation that they would be starting with a blank canvas after 100 years ran counter to the 'official' history and as such must be kept away from the general population. The museum staff was sworn to secrecy, and they knew what would happen if they talked. There were no more prisons, just mind-changing drugs.

A cover story was put out that a video had been found dating back to before the bombs fell but unfortunately, it had disintegrated over time and nothing could be rescued from it. This explanation was accepted by the public but left the Government with a major concern. They had created their museum bunker from a random choice of the bunker which must imply that this message was repeated in all bunkers. What had happened to the others, is some of the equipment from other bunkers still in working order? Will others see the message? This problem was used as a reason for Government to tighten its grip on the population giving it the right to search everywhere and anywhere for what it called contaminated items that had been allowed to escape from the bunkers as they were being dismantled. Many souvenirs were confiscated with the owners being given corrective treatment.

What had happened to Government in the 50 years from 50 NB to 100 NB? After all that had happened, had democracy once again gone out of the window and we are back where we started? We had previously worked on the assumption, that by considering and taking account of the possible long-term consequences of actions taken today, where long-term means centuries, not decades, we will be acting to best ensure a better world in which our children, their children and their children will live.

Now I am not so sure.